BRUISER

BRUISER

NEAL SHUSTERMAN

SCHOLASTIC INC.
New York Toronto London Auckland
Sydney Mexico City New Delhi Hong Kong

ISBN 978-0-545-42391-5

12 11 10 9 8 7 6 5 4 3 2 1   11 12 13 14 15 16/0

Printed in the U.S.A.   40

First Scholastic printing, September 2011

Typography by Joel Tippie

*Dedicated to Gabriela, Melissa,
Natalie, Geneva, and Jim Hebin,
and all my friends at the
American School of Mexico City*

BRUISER

TENNYSON

1) SYMBIOSIS

If he touches her, I swear I'm going to rip out his guts with my bare hands and send them to his next of kin for lunch.

What is my sister *thinking*? This guy—this looooser—has got no business breathing the same air as her, much less taking her out on a date. Just because he asked doesn't mean she has to accept.

"Are you afraid that if you say no, he'll bury you in his backyard or something?" I ask the question over dinner, while I'm still steaming from the news.

My sister, Brontë, gives me a look that says *Excuse me, but I can take care of myself*, and she says, "Excuse me, but I can take care of myself." She learned that look from our mother, God rest her soul. I give Brontë back a look that says *I think not*, and I say, "You gonna eat that piece of pizza?"

Brontë peels off the cheese, throws it on Dad's plate, and

eats the bread. She's on a high-carb diet, which basically means she eats everything that Dad can't on his low-carb diet. It makes them part of an evolved symbiotic relationship. That's science. Just because I'm an athlete doesn't mean I don't have brains.

Mom, God rest her soul, is still on the phone. She's negotiating with the next-door neighbor, hoping to get him to stop mowing his lawn at seven AM on Sunday morning. I don't know why she needs the phone; we can hear the other end of the conversation through the window. In order to get to the point, Mom has to strategically weave around the field, breaking down the neighbor's defenses by talking gossip and being generally friendly. You know—lulling the guy into a false sense of security before going in for the kill. It's such an all-important conversation that Mom had to order a pizza rather than cook. She also had to order it online, since she was already on the phone.

Mom doesn't cook anymore. She does nothing much motherly or wifely anymore since Dad did some unmentionables during his midlife crisis. Brontë and I have become convinced that Mom, God rest her soul, kind of died inside and hasn't come back from the dead yet. We keep waiting, but all we get is Domino's.

"I'm sixteen," Brontë says. "I can spend time with whoever I want."

"As your older brother, it's my sacred duty to save you from yourself."

She brings her fists down on the table, making all the dinner plates jump. "The ONLY reason you're fifteen minutes older than me is because you cut in front of the line, as usual!"

I turn to our father, searching for an ally. "So Dad, is it legal for Brontë to date out of her species?"

Dad looks up from his various layers of pepperoni and breadless cheese. "Date?" he says. Apparently the idea of Brontë dating is like an electromagnet sucking away all other words in the sentence, so that's the only word he hears.

"You're not funny," Brontë says to me.

"No, I'm serious," I tell her. "Isn't he like . . . a Sasquatch or something?"

"Date?" says Dad.

"Just because he's big," Brontë points out, "that doesn't mean he's apelike; and anyway, *you're* the lowest primate in our zip code, Tennyson."

"Admit it—this guy is just one more stray dog for you!"

Brontë growls at me, like one of the near-rabid creatures she used to bring home on a regular basis. Our house used to be a revolving doggy door, until Mom and Dad put their feet down and we became fish people.

"Is this a boy we know?" Dad asks.

Brontë sighs and gnaws her cheeseless pizza in frustration.

"His name is Brewster Rawlins, and he is nothing like what people say about him."

This is not the way to introduce your father to a prospective boyfriend, and I figure maybe Dad might be terrified enough to forbid her to date him.

"Exactly what do people say about him?" Dad asks. Dad always begins sentences with the word *exactly* when he suspects he doesn't want to hear the answer. I snicker, knowing that Brontë is stuck; and she punches me on the shoulder.

What do they say about the Bruiser? I think. *What don't they say?* "Let's see . . . in eighth grade he was voted Most Likely to Receive the Death Penalty."

"He's *quiet*," says Brontë. "He's *inscrutable*, but that doesn't mean he's a bad person. You know what they say: Still waters run deep—"

"—and are full of missing persons."

Brontë hits me on the shoulder again. "Next time," she says, "I'll use your lacrosse stick."

"Inscrutable . . . ," Dad says, mulling over the word.

"It means 'hard to understand,'" shouts Mom from across the room as if he didn't know. Mom never passes up a good opportunity to make Dad look stupid.

"Your mother," grumbles Dad, "knows full well that *inscrutable* was one of *my* words."

"Nope," says Mom, "it was one of mine."

They're referring to the vocabulary curse Brontë and I have been under since kindergarten. Mom and Dad alternate in force-feeding us one power word every day, which we are expected to swallow without vomiting. That's what you get when both of your parents are professors of literature. That, and being named after dead writers. Very aberrant, if you ask me (Mom's word). As teachers, however, they should have realized that Tennyson Sternberger would not fit on a Scantron.

"The Bruiser comes from a screwed-up family," I tell Dad. "They're a bunch of nut jobs."

"Oh," says Brontë, "and we're not dysfunctional?"

"Only your father," says Mom. "But apparently he's taken care of it."

Mom could have been a great sniper if she had chosen that line of work. Every time she gets off a nice one, it gives me hope that her soul might be reviving.

As for the Bruiser, he has no mother. No father either. No one knows what the deal is there. All people know is that he lives with his uncle and an eight-year-old brother who looks like he's being raised by wolves. And this is the family Brontë wants to date into. My sister obviously was never visited by the common sense fairy.

"Exactly when were you planning to see this boy?" Dad asks.

"He's taking me miniature golfing on Saturday afternoon."

"Real high-class," I say.

"You shut up!"

And I do, because now I know everything I need to know about her so-called date.

2) CONSOLATION

I take my girlfriend, Katrina, to play miniature golf Saturday afternoon. Is it coincidence, or is it design? You tell me.

"Must we?" she asks when I suggest it.

"We must," I answer, and offer no further explanation. Her hatred of miniature golf, I think, is born of the fact that her father golfed away her entire childhood instead of spending it at home. I suppose Wackworld Miniature Golf Emporium is a reminder of those dark times.

"It's a happy place," I tell her. "You can't hate Wackworld; it's like hating Disneyland."

"I hate Disneyland," she says, although she won't tell me why. Actually, I'm afraid to find out.

"Okay, I'll go," she tells me, "as long as we don't keep score." And since my motives have nothing to do with golfing competition, I agree.

"You're paying, right?" Katrina asks. "Because I will not pay money to hit a ball with a stick."

I tell her that I'll pay, but she really didn't need to ask because I always pay. Katrina's very old-school when it comes to dating. The guy always pays, and holds doors for her, and pulls out chairs. I actually kind of like it; it's cool pretending to be a gentleman.

Katrina and I had begun as what you might call a consolation couple. In other words, she really wanted to go out with my friend Andy Beaumont, and I really wanted to go out with her friend Stacy VerMoot. But Andy and Stacy found each other, and have since become surgically attached at the hip. That left Katrina and me as each other's consolation prize. As I had just dislocated my shoulder and Katrina wants to be a nurse, it all just popped into place.

"Life," my father had once said, "is all about settling." Unfortunately, he'd said that right in front of Mom, who proceeded to serve him a peanut butter and onion sandwich for dinner that night.

"Life is all about settling," she reminded him as she slipped the plate in front of him. His response had been to eat the whole horrific sandwich out of spite, then catch her unawares with a big, slobbery, peanut butter and onion kiss. After that they didn't speak to each other for about a day and a half. I swear, parents can be such children.

I meet Katrina at her house, and we walk to Wackworld,

since buses in our corner of suburbia don't go anywhere but to some place called the Transportation Center, where you can catch a dozen other buses that don't go anywhere. Since I'm still not old enough for a license, my only choices are bike, parental taxi, or my own two feet. Katrina always prefers walking, because it provides us with an opportunity to talk. Actually, it provides *her* with an opportunity to talk and me with the opportunity to listen. The only time those roles reverse is after a lacrosse game, when you can't shut me up.

". . . so for the entirety of math class," Katrina continues, "Miss Markel has one of her false eyelashes dangling half on, half off her left eye, like a caterpillar; and the whole class is watching and waiting for the thing to drop. . . ."

I don't mind her stories anymore. When we first started going out, I would zone out when she got into it; but as time went on, I got used to it and actually found that I enjoyed listening.

". . . I don't know why she wears false lashes; I guess it must be a generational thing, like the way some women pluck out their eyebrows, then paint on fake ones, or like foot binding in India—"

"China."

"Right, and I think she wears a wig, too. So anyway, she finally turns her head real fast and off the eyelash flies, and where does it land? Right on the head of Ozzy O'Dell—who had just shaved all his body hair for swimming, including his head; and since the thing still has a little glue, it sticks there on top of his scalp, like a teeny-tiny Mohawk, and he doesn't even know. . . ."

The thing about Katrina is that her voice is kind of hypnotic, like a spiritual chant in some foreign language.

". . . so tell me, how was I supposed to focus on a math quiz with Mini-Mohawk Ozzy sitting in front of me, the thing flapping in the breeze from the open window?"

"Did Markel ever notice it?"

"Yeah, like five minutes before the end of class she saw it, quietly plucked it from his head, then slipped it into her desk drawer, thinking no one saw, even though everyone did—but by then it was too late to get my quiz done, so the whole thing was a crash and burn of epic proportions, and all because of a stupid fake eyelash."

Katrina's life is very dramatic. Maybe my sister thinks that by going out with the Bruiser she'll have drama, too; but I know guys better than she knows guys, and knowing *that* guy, I think she's in for something more in the horror genre.

3) COERCION

The entrance to Wackworld Miniature Golf Emporium is marked with a massive sign all done in bright red letters on a very serious black background. The sign warns of all the activities that are not allowed. Every few months a new item gets added as visitors come up with amazing new activities to threaten life, limb, and property. Any time I go there, I make a point of reading the sign to find out what new things have been added. Here are my personal favorites:

> *Do not fill the fountain with alcohol, gasoline, or other flammable substances!*

> *Attaching children to the arms of the windmill by means of staple gun or other such devices is strictly prohibited!*

Toads, turtles, and other small animals may not be substituted for golf balls!

Please do not paint genitalia on the mermaids!

I am proud to say that I was responsible for the addition of that last one a few years back.

As we enter through the gate, I scan the rolling hills of concrete and artificial turf until finding Brontë and the Bruiser. They're on hole three but have moved on to hole four by the time Katrina negotiates herself an acceptable club and demands a red ball from the ball shack geek.

"Why red?" I ask.

"Easier to spot," she says. "Besides, red is the new black."

"I thought pink was the new black."

"Yes, but red is the new pink."

I point at my shirt. "What does that say for green?"

"It only gets worse for green." Then she hits her ball; it smacks the windmill blade and comes flying back at us.

"I hate windmills," says Katrina.

"You and Don Quixote."

"Who?"

"Never mind." I suffer the constant scourge of literary parents. Thank God I'm good at sports, or I might have been pegged early in life and beaten up in hallways. Life is cruel.

We putt our way through the first hole. Just ahead of us, a slow-moving family allows us to play through. I get a hole in one, and that speeds us along. Now Brontë and the Bruiser are only two holes ahead.

"Hey," says Katrina, "isn't that your sister?"

"Oh, yeah, I guess it is."

"Who's that she's with?"

I just shrug and continue playing. We both make a quick par three, and we've closed the gap down to one hole.

Up ahead, Brontë has spotted me. I give her a grin and a little wave. She sends me back a chilly glare that could end global warming.

"Hi, Brontë," Katrina says as we finally intercept them.

"What a surprise!" I say.

"Yeah," grumbles Brontë, "some surprise."

I look at the Bruiser—this is the first time I've ever been this close to him. He's big. Not just big but hulking. At sixteen he's got all this goat hair under his chin and wispy sideburns. His hair is dark, and neglected. You can tell he tried to comb it, but you can also tell he gave up halfway through. He looks like a vagrant in training. I hate him. I hate the concept of him. He's a freight train of bad news barreling at my sister.

"Hey, can we join you guys," Katrina asks, "and make it a foursome?"

The Bruiser shrugs like he doesn't care; and Brontë throws up her hands, giving up all hope of getting rid of me. "Sure," she says miserably, "why not."

"You haven't introduced me to your friend," I say, all daisies and sunshine.

Brontë looks like she might become physically ill. "Brewster, this is my brother, Tennyson. Tennyson, this is Brewster."

"Hey," says the Bruiser, shaking my hand. His eyes are an ugly pea green, and his huge hand is greasy, the way your hand gets after you've eaten a bag of chips. After shaking, I wipe my hand on my pants. He notices. I'm glad.

Katrina narrows her eyes at him, studying him. "I've got a class with you, haven't I?" She knows the Bruiser but just doesn't recognize him out of his natural environment.

"English," he says in a dead, flat voice. This guy is the king of one-word answers—probably all his brain can hold at one time. He sets for his shot. It's almost comical; his golf club is much too small for him, as is his shirt—either he outgrew it, or it shrunk a few sizes after he got it. The overall effect is very Winnie-the-Pooh, without the pot belly or cuteness. He hits the ball too hard, it bounces off the course, and it gets swallowed by a topiary hedge shaped like a walrus.

"Tough break," I say. "That'll cost ya."

"It's only a game," he grumbles, then lumbers off in search of his ball. Katrina smacks her next ball and follows it to the far end of the hole, leaving me alone with Brontë, who gets in my face the second Katrina is out of earshot.

"You are going to pay for this in the worst way!" Brontë

snarls. "I haven't figured out how; but when I do, you will suffer."

I look toward the walrus bush. "I think your date was distracted by something shiny. I'd better go help him find his ball." I saunter off, leaving her fuming.

He's around the other side of the huge walrus bush, fighting pine branch flippers to get at his ball, poking the club into the shrub. I get in there right beside him, force my way deep into the branches, and snatch up his ball. I hold it out to him, and he reaches for it; but instead of giving it to him, I grab him by his shirt, pulling him close to me, and I hiss in his face.

"I don't care what you think is going on between you and my sister, but it's not happening, *comprende*? My sister doesn't know what you're all about, but I do."

He looks at me with dumb hate in his swampy eyes but says nothing.

"Am I getting through that rock skull of yours, or do I have to pound it in through your ears?"

"Get your hands off me."

I grip his shirt a little harder. I think maybe I've got some chest hairs in there, but he doesn't show the pain. "Sorry, I didn't hear you."

"I said, Get your stinking hands off me or I'm gonna find a new use for this golf club."

That's just the kind of thing I'm expecting to hear from a

guy like this. I don't let him go. "Let's see what use you've got in mind," I say.

He doesn't do anything. I didn't think he would. Finally I let him go. "Stay away from my sister," I tell him.

He grabs the ball from my hand and strides back to Brontë. "I don't feel like playing anymore," he says, and stalks off with Brontë hurrying behind him. She throws me a gaze of pure, unadulterated hatred, and I wave. My mission of coercion is accomplished.

Katrina, who did not care for the way she played this hole, claims herself a do over. She comes up beside me and watches the retreat of my sister and the Swamp Thang. "Where are they going?"

"Their separate ways," I say. Katrina swings, and her ball bounces up, wedging in the miniature girders of the Eiffel Tower.

"I hate the Eiffel Tower," she says, and I smile at her, secretly relishing my victory.

Sometimes you have to take control of a situation. Sometimes you have to be the dominant force; otherwise chaos becomes law. I mean, look at lacrosse. This is a game that started as Native American warfare, with warriors breaking their enemies' bones with their sticks as they carried the ball for miles. Even soccer was played with human heads once upon a time. It took the brute force of civilization to tame all that into lawful competition. But one look at the

Bruiser and you know that there's nothing lawful about him. The fact that Brontë can't see that scares me, because there will come a time when I can't protect her . . . and what if someday she finds out the hard way about guys who still see life as head-kicking warfare. You hear stories all the time.

So hate me all you want, Brontë, for what I did here; but that will pass—and someday, if we're lucky, we'll both look back at this day and you'll say "Thank you, Tenny, for caring enough to protect me from the big and the bad."

4) REVELATION

Brontë comes into my room that night, grabs me by the shoulders, and pushes me back onto my bed so hard, my head hits the wall.

"Ow!"

"You're pond scum!" she says to me.

I don't deny the charge, but sometimes pond scum prevails.

"What did you say to him behind the walrus?" she asks.

"I read him his Miranda rights," I told her. "He has the right to remain silent; he has the right to find some other girl to drool over—y' know, the normal things you'd say to a criminal."

"He's never been arrested!" she said. "Those are just stories made up by idiots like you. He's just misunderstood; but I, for one, am making the effort to understand him. He will not give in to your threats; and I will not stop seeing him, no matter how much bullying you do!"

That makes me laugh. "Bullying? Give me a break."

"It's true, Tennyson! You're a bully. You've always been a bully."

"Says who?" I immediately imagine punching out anyone who might call me a bully, and then realize that my own thoughts are proving Brontë's point, which just makes me want to punch someone even more. This is what we call a vicious cycle, and I don't feel all that good about it. I never thought of myself as a bully; and although this isn't the first such accusation, it's the first one that breaks through my defenses and hits home. Suddenly I realize that maybe, in some people's eyes, I am. This is what we call a revelation. Revelations are never convenient, and always annoying.

"Stay away from Brewster!" she warns me, then she turns to leave; but I don't let her go.

"I get it, okay?" I tell her. She lingers by the door. "He's the first boy you like who likes you back, so it feels kind of special. I get it."

She turns to me, some of her steam cooling in the kettle. "He's not the first," she says. "Just the first in my adult life."

I find it funny that we're the same age, give or take a quarter of an hour, and yet she considers herself an adult.

"Be careful, Brontë . . . because you have to admit, this guy is kind of . . . *beneath* you."

She looks at me before she leaves, sadly shaking her head. "*You* be careful, Tenny. Being a snob can make a person very, very ugly."

5) FACTOIDS

I never considered myself a bully. I never considered myself a snob. But then, who does? There's a way to objectively analyze it. All you have to do is look at the facts.

Fact #1) I'm reasonably smart. I'm no genius, but I get good grades without ever having to try. It really ticks off the kids who have to study their brains out to make the grade. It's not like I brag about it, but my mere existence is enough to breed resentment in certain circles.

Fact # 2) I'm coordinated. Not my fault either, I just came that way. It made it easier for me to excel at sports when I was a kid and to build the skills to be a contender in quite a few of them.

Fact #3) I'm reasonably decent looking. I'm no pretty boy, and I don't have six-pack abs or anything; but when it comes to looks, confidence counts for a lot, and I'm nothing if not confident. Between you and me, I think I project a lot better looking than I actually am.

Fact #4) We're not exactly hurting for money. We're by no means rich, but we don't go hungry either. Both Mom and Dad have tenure at the university and pull in decent salaries. They drive modest but respectable cars, and I suspect that when Brontë and I start driving, we'll both get our own modest but respectable cars.

So, does all this make me a snob? Is it wrong for me to think that the Bruiser, with his creepy family and slimy ways, is somehow lower than me? *Yes, it does make you a snob,* I hear Brontë's voice telling me in my head. *It does, Tennyson, because there's a fine line between confidence and arrogance. There's a fine line between being assertive and being a bully. And you're on the wrong side of both lines.*

We're not telepathic twins or anything, but sometimes I wonder because once in a while I have fictional conversations with her. It irks me that, even in my imagination, she can always, always have the last word.

6) DECIMATED

I don't know where my head is at on Monday. Maybe it's because I feel a little bit guilty for being so mean to the Bruiser. Anyway, I do my best to suspend judgment on him; and, for Brontë's sake, I try to keep an open mind.

It's not until the end of the day that I run into him in the most awkward and uncomfortable of situations.

I'm early into the locker room for lacrosse practice, and he's just getting done with PE. He's the last kid there—apparently he doesn't dress with the other kids; he waits until the rest of them are gone.

The instant I see him, I know why.

The first thing I see is his back. It's enough to scare anyone. There's damage there, strange damage. It's impossible to tell what has caused it. Scars and pockmarks; discolorations; a big bruise on his shoulder, yellowed around the edges. His back is decimated, like the cratered surface of the moon.

I just stand there staring. He slips on his shirt, not even knowing that I'm there. Then he turns around and catches me watching him. He knows I've seen his back. I stare for a moment too long.

"What do *you* want?" he asks without looking me in the eye.

I want to match his nasty tone, but I know I have to curb my bully/snob factor. Letting something like that run unchecked will turn you into a creep. My one saving grace is that true creeps don't ever know they are; and if I'm worried about becoming one, maybe it means I won't. The only thing I can think of to say is "So what kind of name is Brewster? Were you named after someone?"

He looks at me like it's a trick question. "What do you care?"

"I don't. I'm just wondering."

He doesn't answer me; he just puts on his jacket: a beat-up leather bomber that looks like it has actually seen several generations of war. Still, the scars on the jacket are nothing compared to what I saw on his back. "Cool jacket," I say. "Where'd you get it?"

"Thrift store," he answers.

I hold back the urge to say "It figures," and instead I just say, "Cool."

He stands facing me now, shoulders squared. Gunslinger

position. It's a stance that says "C'mon, I dare you." He doesn't trust me, but that's just fine. I don't trust him either. I can't even say I dislike him any less; but now I'm curious and worried, and not just for Brontë but maybe a little bit for him, too. Who could do things like that to his body and get away with it, especially to a guy as big as him?

"So, what is it you want?" he asks, "because I got things to do."

"Who says I want anything?" That's when I realize that I'm in gunslinger position, too, blocking his way out. I step aside to let him pass. I think he expects me to trip him, or kick him or something. I wonder if he's disappointed when I don't.

"My great-grandfather," he says as he passes. "That's who I was named after."

And he's gone, just as a bunch of kids from my lacrosse team enter.

7) RECEPTACLE

Our parents never spanked us. They come from the brave new world of time-out and positive reinforcement.

I've always been a very physical kid, though, always using my fists or my body as a battering ram. I can't tell you how many times I've been hauled into the principal's office for fighting. I've given my share of black eyes and bloody noses and gotten my share of them as well—and playing lacrosse, well, there's never a time when I don't have some bruise on my body, somewhere.

But the kind of things I saw on the Bruiser made his nickname hit home for me. None of those marks could be explained away innocently. He didn't get that way from fighting, or from sports. He got that way from being the human receptacle of someone else's brutality.

8) OBTUSE

Mom teaches a class on nineteenth-century realism on Monday nights, so that's Dad's night to not cook. He orders fast food just as skillfully as Mom does. The three of us sit at the dinner table eating KFC on flimsy paper plates with plastic sporks. Whoever invented the spork should be killed. Dad peels the breading from his chicken and gives it to Brontë, allowing her to savor all eleven herbs and spices that make it so finger-lickin' good.

"I saw the Bruiser today," I tell Brontë as we eat. "Brewster, I mean."

"And how did you torment him?" she snaps.

I don't take the bait. Instead I say, "It was in the locker room. He had his shirt off." I take a bite of my chicken, chew, and swallow. "Have you ever seen him with his shirt off?"

Dad looks up from his skinless chicken and talks with his

mouth full. "Exactly why would she have seen him with his shirt off?"

"Oh, puh-lease!" she says to him. "Let's not get out the heart paddles, Dad; he's never been bare chested in my presence." Now Brontë turns her attention to me, studying me, trying to figure out what sinister maneuver I'm working here. The truth is, I'm just curious as to what she knows, or at least what she suspects.

"Why would you ask that question?" she says; but since I don't know any more than what I saw, I don't want to tell her.

"Never mind," I say, "it's not important." I try unsuccessfully to scrape the last of the mashed potatoes from the bottom of the Styrofoam cup with my spork.

"You are so obtuse!" Brontë says, exasperated.

I am calm in my response. "Do you mean stupid, or angular? You need to be more specific with your insults."

"Jerk!"

"No thanks," I tell her. "I much prefer the Colonel's seasonings to Jamaican spice."

It probably would be in my best interests to leave Brontë alone for the rest of the night and not push things, but I can't do that. After dinner I go up to Brontë's room. Her door is open, but still I knock timidly. I'm never timid, but tonight I am.

Brontë must notice because she looks up at me from

her homework, and her standard expression of annoyance changes. Now she looks curious, maybe even a little concerned, because she asks, "What's wrong?"

I shrug. "Nothing. I just wanted to talk to you about Brewster."

"I don't want to talk to you," Brontë says.

"I know," I say to her, "but I think you should listen."

She crosses her arms, clearly ready to dismiss anything I say.

"You know where he lives, right?" I ask.

"He lives in a house," Brontë says, "just like we do."

"And have you met his family? His uncle, I mean, the one he lives with?"

"Where are you going with this?" Brontë asks.

"Does he talk about his uncle?"

"No," says Brontë.

"Maybe you should ask him." Then I leave it in her hands and turn to go; but when I glance back, I can see her staring at her homework, pencil in hand but doing no work. Good. She's thinking about it. I don't know what she'll do, but she's thinking about it. I don't even know what I want her to do.

9) DETERIORATING

Our neighborhood has the distinction of being one of the fastest-growing planned communities in the state. Look at an empty field, now blink; and when you open your eyes, there's a whole housing development there. Blink again; this time there's a new mall right next to it. I can imagine farmers staring, bewildered, at a jungle of pink stucco and red-tile roofs, wondering how their cornfield became a subdivision while they weren't looking. In reality those farmers sold their plots of land for ridiculous prices and made out like bandits, so I can't feel sorry for them. But then there are whole plots of land where the owners held out for more money and missed the boat.

The Bruiser lives in such a place. It had once been a small farm, but it hadn't been cultivated for a long time. Crops had long ago given way to a wild field of weedy brush, a deteriorating eyesore amid the perfectly manicured lawns of our little neighborhood.

There's a bull on the property, old and a little too tired to be cranky. It seems to serve no purpose, not even to itself. Occasionally kids will torment it on the way to school. It'll snort, make like it's going to charge the fence, and then give up, realizing that it's not worth the effort. I imagine the Bruiser is somewhat like that bull.

The day I follow the Bruiser home is the day the bull dies.

10) INTERCESSION

I'm not exactly what you would call stealthy, but the Bruiser isn't all that observant either, so I'm able to follow him all the way home. I don't know what I expect to find, but curiosity is rarely rational. Besides, it's easy to tell myself that it's more than just curiosity. It's what lawyers call "due diligence"— necessary research—and I'm not even doing it for myself; it's for Brontë's sake, although if she knew I was tailing her boyfriend, she'd rip me a new digestive tract.

Even though I know where he lives, I want to observe what he does. Are there other kids he meets up with on the way home? A drug dealer, maybe? I promise myself I won't jump to any conclusions, but I keep my eyes open for anything out of the ordinary.

He makes no contact with anyone today. He's a true loner, deep in his own thoughts, whatever they might be. He glances behind him once; but we're separated by a few groups of other kids, keeping me camouflaged. Although I have my lacrosse stick with me, I keep it low, because if he spots that, it'll draw his attention and he'll see that I'm the one holding it.

His property—about an acre—is surrounded by a tall chain-link fence, and an alley runs beside the fence like a concrete moat separating modern suburbia from the weedy little patch of uncultivated farmland. Across the alley is a strip mall, complete with a supermarket, an ice-cream shop, a Hallmark, and a place called Happi Nails, where I assume women go to make their nails happy. Dumpsters stand in the alley up against the Bruiser's property fence like dark green barricades erected to keep out his world.

The Bruiser opens a rusted gate that bears a NO TRESPASS-ING sign and latches it behind him, then crosses through the weeds toward his house. I follow along in the adjacent alley and peer between two of the Dumpsters. Looking through that rusted chain-link fence is like looking into a whole other time and place. The old one-story farmhouse is more like a shack. There's a big, rusted propane tank, and the farmhouse roof is shedding shingles. The building seems to list, as if it has shifted off its foundation. The place is painted a color that I think was once green but has since faded to various shades that have no specific name on the color spectrum. And the smell of the place . . . well, it smells like bull and the stuff a bull leaves behind. I pity the neighbors downwind.

Today, however, the lone bull on the farm isn't very active. In fact, it doesn't look right at all. I don't know much about livestock, but if a large animal is lying on its side with its head at a funny angle and its eyes open, chances are it's not taking a nap.

I watch it for a long time waiting for it to move, but it doesn't; and now I know something's wrong, because the Bruiser's just standing there staring at it with the same dumb expression I must have on my own face. That's when his brother comes out onto the porch.

Snapshot of kid brother:

Bare feet, torn jeans, and a striped shirt that's as faded as the wood slats of the old farmhouse. He's got a runny nose I can see glistening all the way from here, and dirty blond hair where the "dirty" actually means dirty. Flocks of birds could make their nest in there and no one would know, and I'm only slightly exaggerating. This kid is the definition of "feral child."

So the kid comes out onto the porch, all snot nosed and teary eyed, and says to the Bruiser, "Tri-tip is sick, Brew. You can help him, right?"

The Bruiser just stands there looking at the bull and finally, slowly, turns to his brother. "Nothing's gonna help him, Cody."

"No!" says Cody. "No! Don't say that; he's just sick is all. You can fix it; you always fix it!"

"I'm sorry, Cody," says the Bruiser; and then, all tears and drama, Cody races to the deceased bull, throws himself on it, and tries to give it a weird, awkward hug, but his arms can't reach around the thing.

"No, no, no!" Cody cries.

Maybe I should be feeling something here—some sort of sadness—because, after all, this is clearly a beloved pet; but it's all so weird. It's like I'm watching the psychotic version of *Old Yeller*, where the dead dog has been digitally replaced by this sorry old bull with lonely eyes that stare at me from across the field. Eyes that seem to be asking, "Do I really need this?"

That's when the third and final family member comes out onto the porch.

Portrait of the Bruiser's uncle:

Well-worn pointy boots, a tarnished belt buckle about half the size of a hubcap, tentaclelike tattoos that disappear up into his shirtsleeves, gray wispy hair, and bristly beard stubble. By the way he holds on to the doorframe as he steps out, I can tell he's either drunk or hungover. I want to scream at him, "Don't you know you're a walking stereotype?" The bitter, aging redneck. I'm sure his name is something like Wyatt or Clem: a wannabe cowboy whose cow just dropped dead.

As if to acknowledge my assessment, the man flicks a cigarette butt and says, "I shoulda sold that bull for dog food years ago."

"Don't say that, Uncle Hoyt!" wails Cody.

"You see what I've gotta put up with?" Uncle Hoyt says to the Bruiser. "You see?" As if it's all the Bruiser's fault. "Where you been? How come you're not home on time?"

"I *am* home on time." Then the Bruiser asks his uncle, "When did it happen?"

"How the hell should I know?"

Over by the bull, Cody continues to wail. "It's not true. . . . It's not true. . . ."

"Will you shut him up?" demands Uncle Hoyt.

The Bruiser moves to his brother and pries him away from the dead bull; but the kid goes ballistic, screaming and cursing and fighting and kicking, limbs flailing like a spider monkey.

"Cody, stop it!" the Bruiser yells; but the kid's gone into demonic possession mode, scratching and biting until it's all the Bruiser can do just to peel him off himself. And the second he does, Cody jumps back on the bull, clinging to it like cellophane and bawling even more loudly than before.

That's when Uncle Hoyt reaches down, undoes his belt buckle, and in a single move pulls his belt out of his pants, wrapping the end of it around his palm like it's something he does on a regular basis. He storms toward the boy, buckle end dangling. "IT'S DEAD!" the man screams. "GET YOUR SNIVELIN' ASS AWAY FROM IT OR I SWEAR I'LL WAIL ON YOUR HIDE TWELVE WAYS TILL DOOMSDAY."

He brings his arm back, threatening to swing the buckle—and the Bruiser doesn't do a thing. He just stands there watching, like he's helpless to stop it.

"No!"

That's my voice. I don't even realize I'm going to shout it until the word's already out of my mouth. I never meant to intercede, but I can't help it. Someone has to stop this.

Suddenly they all turn to me, and now I'm part of the cast of this twisted old Western. I have no choice but to take my place in the scene. I drop my backpack but keep hold of my lacrosse stick. Then I quickly climb the Dumpster and jump over the fence, racing toward the three of them. The moment I'm close enough, I raise my lacrosse stick as a weapon, perhaps the way it was done back in the days when the game was warfare. Then I stare the man in his hateful, rheumy eyes and say, "If you hit that kid, I will take you down!"

And everything freezes like a snow globe. I half expect little flakes to start swimming all around us. Then the Bruiser steps in front of me. He grabs me with his heavy hands, and he whispers angrily into my ear, "Stay out of this!"

I try to pull free from the Bruiser's grasp, but he's just too big. As I struggle, my lacrosse stick falls to the ground.

"Who the hell are you?" Uncle Hoyt finally says now that he's not in imminent danger of having his head bashed in.

The Bruiser pushes me back. "Stay out of this!" he says again. "This isn't any of your business."

"Please, Uncle Hoyt," pleads Cody, "leave Tri-tip alone."

Uncle Hoyt looks at me, sizing me up. "This a friend of yours?" he asks the Bruiser.

"No!" says the Bruiser quickly. "Just some kid from school."

Uncle Hoyt spits on the ground, giving me a dirty look. Then he turns and saunters inside, dragging the belt like that buckle's his pet on a leash. The screen door closes and I can't see him anymore, but I hear him calling from inside: "You dispose of that bull, Brewster. I don't wanna know about it."

The Bruiser stares at me with anger that ought to be directed at his uncle, and now the only sounds are clanking shopping carts from the market beyond the fence and the wails of a little boy clinging to a dead beast that's already collecting flies.

With Uncle Hoyt gone, the Bruiser holds my gaze only a moment more before he decides I'm not worth the effort. Then he goes over to his brother . . . but instead of comforting him, he kneels beside him, puts his hands on the bull just like his brother, and just like his brother he begins to grieve. It starts with mild weeping but soon crescendos into the same tortured sobs as his little brother, both of them wailing in a strange harmony of misery.

I'm embarrassed to be watching—it's as if I'm witnessing something too personal to view—but I can't look away. I want to leave, but it would be like walking out in the middle of a funeral.

A few moments more and Cody's sobbing begins to resolve into whimpers; but the Bruiser is still doubled over in his sorrow, the sobs so intense I can almost feel the ground shake as his chest heaves. In a moment Cody has fully recovered, as if all he needed was someone else to share in his grief.

The Bruiser's anguished sobs go on for at least another minute while Cody waits, patient and untroubled, playing tic-tac-toe in the dirt.

Finally the Bruiser's sobs begin to trail off. He gets control of himself. Then he stands and picks up Cody, who wraps his spidery arms around his big brother's neck. Brewster carries his brother inside without even looking at me once.

I stand there for a while, more than ready to leave yet feeling like there's something left undone. Finally I pick up my lacrosse stick and try to wipe off the mud—at least I hope it's mud. I turn to go, deciding that this was all just one big mistake, when I hear the screen door creak open behind me. I turn to see the Bruiser coming outside again.

"Mind telling me what you're doing here?" he asks.

I'm beyond making up excuses now, beyond caring what comes out of my mouth. And when you don't care what you say, the truth comes with amazing ease. "I was spying on you to find out what's wrong with you and your family."

I expect him to spew something nasty at me, but instead he just sits on the porch steps and says, "Find out all that you wanted to know?"

"Enough," I answer him. "Were you just gonna let your uncle beat on your brother?"

He looks me dead in the eyes. "What makes you so sure he would do it?"

"You don't pull out your belt like that unless you plan to use it."

The Bruiser just shrugs. "How do you know? Do you think you know my uncle better than I do? Maybe he just likes to hear himself yell—did you ever think of that?"

I can't quite figure all of this out, but he's put enough doubt in my mind now so that I can't answer him, which I'm sure is what he wants. But then I remember something.

"I saw your back," I remind him. "I think I can put two and two together."

Now his gaze looks a little angry again. A little scared. "Two and two doesn't always equal four." There's something about his tone of voice—something that says that maybe he's right. Maybe it's not what I think. But there is also something in his voice that says it's worse.

"Anyway," he says, "it was gutsy of you to stand up to Uncle Hoyt like that."

"Yeah, well . . ."

"You wanna come in?" he asks. This I was not expecting.

"Why would I want to do that?"

He shrugs. "I dunno. Maybe to see that we don't live with rats. To see that I'm not building pipe bombs in my basement."

"I never said you were."

"But I bet you thought it."

I look away from him at that. The truth is, from the moment I found out he was dating Brontë, I thought every possible bad thing my imagination could muster up about him. Pipe bombs in the basement were on the milder end of the spectrum.

"C'mon," he said, "I'll get you something to drink."

Maybe it did take guts to stand up to his crazy, belt-wielding uncle, but I think it took more guts for the Bruiser to invite me inside.

11) DÉTENTE

I follow the Bruiser in. I have to say, I'm a little disappointed at what I find. It's just a house. Sure, it's kind of run-down and sparsely decorated, but it's still just a house. The one thing about it, though, is that all the colors are off, just like on the outside. The wallpaper is faded, the sofa has stains on the cushions, the blue carpet is mottled purple and brown in spots. A *bruise*, I think, *the entire house is like one big bruise.*

I can hear a TV playing somewhere deeper in the house. Beyond the kitchen is an arched doorway, dark except for the flickering light of the TV. There must be a family room back there, but somehow I suspect family has little to do with it. I'm sure it's Uncle Hoyt's lair, complete with a deteriorating recliner, a TV with color issues, and empty beer cans multiplying like dust bunnies.

The Bruiser pours me some lemonade. "I promise it's not poisoned," he says.

I don't want to touch anything. Not because it's dirty but because it feels unclean. I can't quite explain the difference, although I suspect it has something to do with my own snob factor. Conflicted, I force myself to sit in a chair at the kitchen table. There are dirty dishes in the sink. He notices me noticing.

"Sorry," he says, "the dishes are *my* job. I usually take care of them when I get home."

"What does your uncle do?" I asked him.

"Road construction," Brewster says. "He works nights, driving a steamroller for the Transportation Authority."

Somehow that doesn't surprise me. I get this image of a maniacal Uncle Hoyt rolling over defenseless wildlife caught in the unset asphalt.

I pick up my glass, and he looks at my knuckles. Four out of five knuckles on my right hand have scabs in various states of healing. "Where'd you get those," he asks, "beating on band geeks?"

He's trying to push my buttons. I don't let him. "Lacrosse," I tell him.

"Right," he says. "Must be a rough sport."

I shrug. "Good for getting out your aggression."

He nods. "What do you do in the off-season?"

"I use the stick to smash mailboxes."

He looks at me like I'm serious.

"I'm kidding," I tell him, but he doesn't seem entirely convinced. I'm uncomfortable with the conversation being all about me, so I flip it back on him.

"So, your uncle's got a government job; he must pull in a decent salary."

The question is right there, although I don't ask it directly: *If he's got a decent job, then why do you live like this?*

The Bruiser glances back toward the family room. The shifting glow from the TV plays on the arched doorway like lightning, making it look like a portal to another dimension. The gateway to Hoyt-Hell: *Abandon all hope ye who enter.* He turns back to me and speaks softly. "My uncle's got an ex-wife and three kids in Atlanta. The government garnishes his wages."

"Garnish," I say. "I thought that was, like, parsley on a dinner plate."

The Bruiser grins. "So there's something I know that you don't?" He relishes the moment before explaining. "Garnishing means the government takes child support right out of his salary even before he gets the check because they know he won't pay it otherwise." The Bruiser thinks about it and shakes his head. "Funny—he runs out on his wife and three kids and then he ends up stuck with Cody and me."

I'm about to ask him how that came to be, but I realize it must not be a pretty story. If they're stuck with a loser uncle, it means that their parents are gone in one way or another. Dead, incarcerated, or AWOL. No joy in any of the possibilities, so I don't ask.

"You're uncle sounds like quite a guy," I say, the sarcasm practically pooling around my ankles, adding another stain to the carpet.

"There are worse things," he says.

Right about now Cody comes out of his room, shirtless.

"My shirt smelled like Tri-tip," he says, "but I got no clean shirts. It's your fault I got no clean shirts!" he tells his brother.

The Bruiser sighs and says to me, "I do the laundry here, too."

I wonder if there are any chores he doesn't do.

When I glance at Cody again, I note that the kid's back is nothing like his brother's. No bruises, no scars, no sign that their short-tempered uncle beats him at all. I begin to wonder if maybe I'm wrong in assuming the man is an abuser. Maybe he just blusters, but he's all wind and no weather. Still, it doesn't answer the question about the Bruiser's back. The Bruiser goes to a little laundry room just off the kitchen and mines through a huge pile of clothes on top of the dryer. He pulls out a small T-shirt and tosses it to Cody.

"Is it clean?"

"No, I wiped my butt on it."

Cody scowls at him, smells the shirt just in case, and

walks away satisfied. He disappears into his room, struggling, Houdini-like, to get his head and arms into the shirt at the same time.

The Bruiser comes back out to join me in the kitchen.

"So, you haven't gotten to the part where you ask me to stay away from your sister. You tried threatening me and that didn't work, so now I figure you're going to try it more respectfully."

I look away from him. I know it might make me seem guilty, but, really, I'm feeling angry at myself for having bullied him in the first place.

"Brontë makes her own decisions," I tell him, then add, "but I won't be happy if she comes anywhere near Uncle Hoyt."

"Neither will I," he says, "and just in case you're worried, I'm not like my uncle."

"I can see that." Then I hold out my hand to him. "So . . . no hard feelings?"

He looks at my hand for a few moments, and I think that maybe there are hard feelings after all; but then he shakes it with a decisive, confident grasp.

We nod to each other—an understanding has been reached, like a détente between two nations that would otherwise be at war.

Then Uncle Hoyt slinks out from his lair, and Brewster withdraws his hand like he's been caught with it in the cookie jar. The man looks at us suspiciously, as if we're plotting against him. "What's he still doing here? Didn't I tell you to get rid of Tri-tip?"

The Bruiser opens his mouth to say something, but I speak first. "What is he supposed to do, snap his fingers and make it go away?"

The man grins, and it's something slimy and nasty. All of a sudden I feel unclean again. "Can't expect you to lift the whole animal at once," he says. "The chain saw's out in the shed."

12) MISDIRECTION

When I get home that night, I don't say anything to Brontë about where I was and what I did that afternoon. Even when she comments at dinner that I smell funny, I just tell her I'll take a shower—even though I've already taken two.

I won't get into the details of Tri-tip's disposal. It was not a pretty sight. I can only thank God there are Dumpsters just on the other side of the Bruiser's fence. Now I understand the close-knit nature of the Mafia, because there's something bonding about disposing of a body.

The next day I see the Bruiser during passing, between second and third periods. We nod to each other an unspoken greeting, almost like it's something secret. He raises a hand to hoist his backpack farther up on his shoulder, and that's when I notice the knuckles on his right hand. Four out of five knuckles are all raw and starting to scab. I figure he must have scraped them up pretty badly during our bull-carving extrava-ganza yesterday afternoon.

Reflexively I look at my own knuckles and notice right away that my scabs are gone. I tend to heal quickly, so I try to dismiss it. After all, how often do I actually look at my knuckles? I get scraped and bruised so much, I don't notice it anymore.

Except that I *did* notice my scabbed knuckles yesterday. The Bruiser and I both did.

I try to tell myself it's nothing, that it's one of life's simple tricks, just like a stage magician's clever misdirection to keep the audience baffled. Yet deep down I know there's something more going on here. Something truly inexplicable I'm afraid to consider.

BRONTË

13) EMPHATICALLY

My brother's an idiot.

Sure, Tennyson's smart, but he's an idiot in all the other ways that matter. Such as when he forced his way into our miniature golf game and intimidated Brewster just because we went out on a date. It wasn't even an *evening* date; it was a middle-of-the-afternoon date, which as anyone can tell you, is barely a date at all. The problem with Tennyson is that he has to be in control of everything. It's like he's worried the whole world will fall apart if he's not holding it together. He thinks no one can survive without the protection of his iron fist, least of all me.

Well, in spite of what Tennyson might think, I am not entirely void of common sense, thank you very much. I deal with boys far better than he deals with girls. Don't believe me? Then take a nice, long look at his current "relationship" with Katrina, who has the right name, because she's got natural disaster written all over her.

I, on the other hand, know that with any boy it's important to truly get to know him before the dates get serious. Not that I have all that much experience, but I'm blessed with friends who do. Their lives are like caution signs in the road, warning me against all the ill-advised things they have done.

1) From Carly I learned never to go out on a date with the younger brother of the most popular guy in school . . . because he thinks he has something to prove, and he'll try to prove it on you.

2) From Wendy I learned that playing ditsy and stupid will only get you boys who are stupider than you're pretending to be.

3) From Jennifer I learned to avoid any boy with an ex-girlfriend who hates him with every fiber of her being . . . because chances are there's a reason she hates him so much, and you may find out the hard way.

4) From Melanie I learned that, while it's true that guys have one thing on their mind, most are greatly relieved and easier to deal with if you make it emphatically clear right up front that they're not going to get that one thing in the foreseeable future. Or at least not from you. Once that becomes clear, either they go after some girl who never learned the warning signs, or they stick around.

I tried out point number four on a boy last year, and it

worked. His name was Max—my first and only boyfriend before Brew—and we got a whole series of necessary milestones out of the way. First date, first kiss, first conniption fit from my parents for breaking curfew. He got the first suspicious look from my father, and I got the first suspicious look from his mother. With all those firsts out of the way, we were free to live normal lives.

We eventually broke up, of course, because all training-wheel relationships must die if we ever intend to graduate from the sidewalk into the bike lane. We've remained friends, though, which has been very good for him socially (see point #3).

As for me, popularity was never something I worried much about. I've always been as popular as I needed to be with the people I cared about, and fairly well liked, too—if you don't count a handful of evil, insecure Barbies who call me Man-Shoulders because I've got a slightly developed upper body from swim team. I take comfort in knowing that while I often come home with gold around my neck, all the Barbies can ever hope for are rocks on their fingers.

So then, with all that taken into account, I felt I was entirely conscious of the risks, and fully prepared to date Brewster Rawlins.

I was spectacularly wrong.

14) IBEX

As much as I hate to admit it, my brother, Tennyson, was right about what first attracted me to Brewster. It was the stray dog thing.

I've always had a dangerously unguarded place in my heart for strays. There was the time when I was ten and brought home a seriously psychotic shih tzu, which proceeded to attack everyone's ankles, drawing more blood than so little a dog should be capable of doing. We named him Piranha and gave him to an animal rescue center that has a no-kill policy, although later I heard that Piranha almost caused them to change their policy.

Regardless, I've discovered that nine out of ten strays have issues that are not life threatening, so I have no desire to change my ways, thank you very much.

When it came to Brewster Rawlins, he might have had a

home, but he was a stray in every other sense of the word.

It all began the day he showed up in the library.

I was a library aide at the time, which involved a lot of hanging around while the librarian tried to come up with busywork for me to do. I didn't mind, because it gave me time to read, and be among the books. Do you know that if you take the books in an average school library and stretched out all those words into a single line, the line would go all the way around the world? Actually, I made that up, but doesn't it sound like it should be true?

Part of my job was to help other kids find books, because not everyone has a keenly organized mind. Some kids could wander the library for hours and still have no idea how to find anything. For them, the Dewey Decimal System might as well be advanced calculus.

I figured that here was one of those kids, because I found him lurking in the poetry section looking like a deer caught in the headlights. A really big deer—maybe a caribou or an ibex.

"Can I help you find something?" I asked as politely as I could, since I've been known to scare off the more timid wildlife.

"Where's the Allen Ginsberg?" he asked.

It took me by surprise. No one came into our school library looking for Allen Ginsberg. I began to scan the poetry shelf alphabetically. "Is it for an assignment?" I was genuinely curious as to which teacher might assign radical beatnik poetry. Probably Mr. Bellini, who we all secretly believed had his brain fried long ago by various and sundry psychedelic chemicals.

"No assignment," he said. "I just felt like reading Ginsberg again."

That stopped me in midscan. In my experience, there are three reasons why a boy will want to take out a book on poetry:

1) to impress a girl

2) for a class assignment

3) to impress a girl.

So, thinking myself oh-so-smart, I smugly said, "What's her name?"

He looked at me, blinking with those ibex eyes. A nice shade of green, I might add.

"Whose name?" he asked.

At this point I felt embarrassed about having to explain my assumption, so I didn't. "Never mind," I said, then quickly found the book and handed it to him. "Here you go."

"Yeah, this is the one. Thanks."

Still, I found it hard to believe. I mean, Allen Ginsberg is not exactly mainstream. His stuff is out there, even by poetry standards. "So . . . you just want to read it for . . . pleasure?"

"Something wrong with that?"

"No, no, it's just . . ." I knew it was time to give up entirely, as I was truly making a fool of myself. "Forget I said anything. Enjoy the book."

Then he looked down at the book. "I can't really explain it," he said. "It makes me feel something, but I don't have to feel it about some*one*, so I get off easy."

It was an odd thing to say—so odd that it made me laugh. Of course, he didn't appreciate that and turned to leave.

Something inside me didn't want our encounter-among-the-stacks to end like this, so before he reached the end of the aisle, I said, "Did you know Allen Ginsberg tried to levitate the Pentagon?"

He turned back to me. "He did?"

"Yes. He and a whole bunch of Vietnam war protesters encircled the Pentagon, then sat in the lotus position and started meditating on levitating the Pentagon at the same time."

"Did it work?"

I nodded. "They measured a height change of one point seven millimeters."

"Really?"

"No, I made that part up. But wouldn't it be wild if it were true?"

He laughed at that, and now seemed like a reasonable time to hold out my hand invitingly and introduce myself. "Hi, I'm Brontë," I said.

"Yeah, I know." He shook my hand, which almost disappeared

into his. "Probably named after the writers Charlotte and Emily Brontë. I've never read them, but I know the names."

Truth be told, I was actually glad he'd never read the Brontës. That would have made him a little *too* odd. "My parents are professors of literature at the university. My brother, Tennyson, is named after a famous poet."

"He must hate that," he said, "being a meathead and all."

"You know him?"

"By reputation."

Which made sense. My brother's obnoxious reputation precedes him like, oh, say, hail before a tornado. "Actually, he loves his name. It keeps people confused. He likes keeping people confused."

He still hadn't introduced himself. Since he knew my name, I wanted him to think I knew his name, too.

"I'll need your ID card to check out the book," I told him.

He handed it to me, and I glanced at the name quickly as we made our way to the circulation desk. "Well, Brewster, if you want my advice on other poets, let me know."

"I just like the angry ones," he said. "Know any more?"

"Plenty." Which was not entirely true, but I knew angry poetry was highly Googleable.

As he left, I tried to size him up in full view. He was large, but not fat, sloppy—not grungy. His clothes seemed worn, but not stylishly so; they were actually worn, and the legs were short enough to prove they'd been around for at least two inches of growth. And although most boys look pretentious in a distressed leather bomber jacket, it seemed natural on him.

It was then that I made the connection—and made it so powerfully, I almost gasped. Brewster Rawlins. This is the boy they call the Bruiser! Always a little too big to be picked on, a little too mad-creepy to be in anyone's clique. He was always just *there*, through elementary school and middle school, lingering in the background. I'd been in a couple of classes with him over the years, but it had been like we were on different planets.

It was hard to reconcile the memory of that kid with the boy I met that day—but one thing was certain: Brewster was a stray, and someone most definitely needed to take him in.

15) HOWLINGLY

In defiance of Tennyson's campaign to remove Brew from my life, I made every effort to see him as much as possible. All right, I'll admit my motives were mixed, but they didn't stay that way for long. Spite against my brother, compassion for a stray, and general curiosity quickly gave way to something deeper—something more real and maybe even more danger-ous, because when you truly start to care about someone, you become vulnerable to all sorts of things. I think Brew knew that better than anyone.

Our first date at Wackworld was a disaster thanks to Tennyson's meddling, and I was determined that our second date would be a success. But what would that date be? During school that week we saw each other at lunch, and he offered to take me to the movies, as most guys do. The movie-date must have been invented by a guy: no possible way to have a conversation, and a darkened room suitable for other activities. Right.

"We'll get to that," I told him. "Maybe. But for now, how about doing something where I get to see your eyes?"

He started to look a little nervous, and his hands retreated into his pockets. I knew what he was thinking: He thought I wanted to be taken to a restaurant—and I knew enough about him to know that money was an issue.

"I was thinking maybe a picnic," I told him.

He was visibly relieved. "Could be fun," he said, then added, "as long as your brother doesn't come popping out of the picnic basket."

I laughed—a little nervously, because I didn't put it past Tennyson to find some way to sabotage it if he knew. Keep in mind, this was right after the Wackworld incident, so I had every reason to fervently believe Tennyson was the enemy.

"My brother won't know about it," I said.

And he didn't. No one did. That Saturday, as far as anyone in my family knew, I was off to meet some friends at the mall; and since I'm such a bad liar, I made sure it was the truth. I did exactly that; I stayed at the mall with friends for a whole twenty minutes and then took off for the head of Mulligan Falls trail. My backpack was full of sandwiches and condiments, and a blanket. Brew was bringing the beverages—"Considering that your name's Brew, I think it's appropriate," I had told him, although I did have to clarify that I wasn't suggesting he bring beer.

When I arrived at the trailhead he was already there, pacing back and forth, perhaps worrying that I wouldn't show. I said hello, giving him a hug. He smelled very Mennen; just the right amount of mildly scented antiperspirant, which, in my book is far more enticing than a boy who reeks of cologne. I find cologne suspicious. Like carpet deodorizer.

"I had to tell my uncle I'm at Saturday school," he told me, "so that gives us a few hours."

Hearing that surprised me. "Why can't you just tell him the truth?"

"Weekends are family time. He prefers me home." And that's all he said on the subject of his uncle.

We took a look at the trail map. "You sure you want to do this?" he asked. "After all, I *was* voted Most Likely to Receive the Death Penalty."

"Oh . . . you heard about that?" I felt a bit embarrassed to be part of a student body that would behave so hurtfully. It never made it into the yearbook, but everyone knew about it.

"Actually," I told him, "I feel safer with you than with most other boys in school."

"Thanks . . . I think."

We took the trail up and out of our community. Housing developments disappeared behind towering trees, and in just a few minutes it felt like we were hours from civilization. It had been an exceptionally wet winter, and the falls were so powerful with the spring thaw, we could already hear the roar even though we were still half a mile away.

"So, tell me something I don't know about you," I asked as we walked. I tried to make eye contact with him, but the question made him self-conscious, and he looked away.

"What kind of thing?"

"Anything," I said. "That you have webbed feet or a vestigial tail. That you're color blind, or a sleepwalker, or an alien lulling humanity into a false sense of security."

I thought he'd laugh, but instead he just said, "I'm none of those things. Sorry." He helped me over a jagged boulder, thought for a moment, then said, "I've got a photographic memory, though."

"Really!" It was much more interesting than any of the things I had suggested, except maybe for the alien—but all things considered, I much preferred that he be terrestrial anyway. "So if you've got a photographic memory, by now you must know the poems in that Allen Ginsberg book by heart." I was just kidding, but a moment later he launched into "Howl," reciting it word for word. And this is no short piece—it's one of those poems that goes on forever. I was impressed, but also unsettled, because, like he said, he liked angry poetry, and "Howl" is a regular fury-fest. Rage against the establishment and all that. As he spat out the words, they became more and more caustic, like a volcanic blast. I imagined I could see superheated steam venting into the air around him as he spoke.

Then when he got to the part about drinking turpentine in Paradise Alley, he forced himself to stop. He was out of breath, like he had just run a sprint. I could tell he was still marginally volcanic inside, but he quelled it quickly.

At that point any other girl would have said, "Thank you, it's been interesting," then shot up a rescue flare. But I'm not any other girl. "Very impressive," I said, then added, "*Howlingly* so."

"Sorry I got a little carried away." He took a deep breath and released it. "Sometimes I feel things very deeply, y'know?"

"How deeply?" I asked.

"Bottomless, kinda."

And I believed it, too. There was something about his sheer intensity, and the way he could harness it, that captivated me. Controlled danger. A safely chained extreme. Was anger the only emotion he experienced so powerfully, or was it that way with everything?

I found myself leaning forward to kiss him. Why, you may ask? Well, don't ask, because I don't have an answer—I just couldn't stop myself. It was just a peck, really, and I moved so quickly that our teeth bumped. Not exactly romantic in the traditional sense of the word, but I don't think traditional was in either of our vocabularies.

He was stunned for a moment, then said something he probably hadn't meant to say out loud. "You're a very strange girl."

"Thank you," I said. "I try."

I turned to continue down the path, but I'll admit I was partially stunned myself, because I didn't look where I was going. My foot slipped on a boulder, got wedged in a crevice, and I went down. I felt a sharp, searing pain in my ankle even before I hit the ground, and I yelped. My blanket-stuffed backpack kept the rest of me from getting hurt, but the rest of me didn't matter if my ankle was out of commission.

"Are you okay?" Brew hurried over to me as I freed my foot with a pained yowl that made a flock of birds take flight.

"No!" I shouted, my frustration overtaking the pain. "I'm not okay!" It wasn't just that the day would be ruined; there was a huge swimming tournament coming up, and ankle troubles are just as bad for a swimmer as they are for any other athlete. "This can't happen now! I can't have a sprained ankle!"

"Let me see." Brew knelt down. By now the sharpness of the pain had subsided—it didn't hurt when I didn't move—but I could feel heat and pressure around my ankle. It was already beginning to swell, and Brew said, "I'll bet it's not sprained; you probably just twisted it."

"Don't touch it!"

"I'll be careful." He gingerly took off my shoe and then my sock. I held on to the hope he was right and that it wasn't as bad as it felt. He held my foot and rotated it to the left.

"Ouch!"

"Sorry."

Then he rotated it more gently to the right. "Better?"

"A little."

"I know some acupressure points," he said as he massaged my foot and ankle. "How does that feel?"

"I don't know," I said. But that was a lie. It felt good. Better than good. I watched as his fingers moved confidently across the bruising skin, caressing the bone beneath and stroking the tendons. A strange and powerful feeling of well-being radiated from my foot out to the rest of me.

"It's called reflexology," he said. "Some people believe the feet are the mirrors of the soul."

I nodded. At that moment he could have said the earth was made of chocolate pudding and I would have believed it. I could swear I felt his heartbeat in the tips of his fingers, but maybe it was mine—and I realized that this was well beyond anything that should be attempted on a second date.

Brew rotated my ankle again.

"How's that?"

"Better." It tingled, it felt a little bit numb, but it didn't hurt. It was more like the feeling you get when you hit your funny bone. In a moment the sensation began to go away.

Then he let go. "Like I said, you just twisted it. You'll be fine."

I stood up and put some weight on it. He was right. I'd been lucky.

"But just in case," he said as he stood up, "maybe we should have our picnic here instead of hiking anymore."

"But . . . but what about the falls? And we haven't even gotten up to the good views."

"It's okay," he said, and offered a little grimace. "To be honest, I've outgrown these shoes—and they're not exactly hiking shoes anyway. They really hurt."

He took a couple of limping, grimacing steps, and I grinned. "You think I don't know what you're doing?" I said. "You're just trying to make me feel better about not making it to the falls."

He shook his head. "No, I'm serious."

He limped and grimaced a little bit more. I could see that he was sticking to his story, so I decided not to argue. I took the blanket and spread it out in a clearing, and we had our picnic.

We talked as we ate and drank, and had a truly wonderful time. It felt good, and I didn't want it to end. I'm not going to be so stupidly sentimental as to say we were suddenly in love or anything, but something did happen that day. Somehow we had become linked. Entwined. It was out of the ordinary, and out of my control.

That's when I realized that I had been wrong from the start: Brewster wasn't a stray at all. If anyone was lost, it was me; and I could feel nothing but gratitude at having been found.

16) KEELHAULED

It took a day for that strange feeling to fade, although it never wore off entirely. Eventually I was able to hurl enough reason at it to camouflage it against a background of protective logic. It was hormones. It was adrenaline. It was the endorphins released by the acupressure. There was nothing out of the ordinary going on at all, and I was entirely in control of the situation. Right.

The following Sunday I invited Brew to join me swimming, and things took a troubling turn.

On weekends our school opens the pool to the public. It's an outdoor pool, even though we live in a geographically iffy part of the country when it comes to weather. Why? Because some über-genius decided it was cheaper to heat an outdoor pool through the winter than to put a building around it. In early April few people come to the pool on Sundays, except the diehards. That was fine. I figured it would give Brew and me some space. The rumor mill was cheerfully rolling out reams about us; and I, for one, didn't want to feed it more pulp by making a grand and glorious public showing among the masses. Knowing that Brew's dictatorial uncle worked a night-shift kind of life, I planned it for morning, when he'd be asleep.

"I watch my brother on Sundays," Brew told me when I suggested it. I told him to bring his brother along.

"I don't have a bathing suit that fits," he said. I told him shorts were fine.

"What if it rains?" he asked. I told him he didn't have to come if he didn't want to.

"No . . . no, I want to come." And there was genuine enthusiasm in his voice when he said it. I was relieved, because the way he was trying to worm out of coming made me worried that he had changed his mind about going out with me. Maybe the ankle massage had been one step too close for him. Maybe he now saw me as the flytrap ready to spring closed around him. But he *did* want to come, and he meant it.

I had just finished swimming my laps when they arrived. Now, the only other person in the pool was one of the regulars—an old lady I call the Water Lily due to her flowery bathing suit and the way that when you look at her, she never seems to be moving forward, like she had somehow taken root in the pool tiles and all that dog paddling was for naught.

Brew was still favoring one foot as he walked, a whole week

after the hike, and I remember thinking how one day in bad shoes can ruin you for a week.

I swam to the edge of the pool to greet Brew and his brother and peeled off my swim cap, because it's not humanly possible to look good in a swim cap. Then I did a quick drop to the bottom and pushed off to the surface so that my hair became a shimmering waterfall instead of a tatty ball of nastiness.

"This is Cody," Brew said. "Cody, this is Brontë." I reached out of the pool to shake the boy's hand. He looked up at the snarling dinosaur painted on the wall behind the pool—our school mascot—and read the team name beneath it. "Are you a raptor?" he asked.

"No," I told him. "I'm a Brontë-saurus."

He laughed at that. Then he removed several layers of mismatched clothes until he was down to his bathing suit and leaped wildly into the pool without even checking the water—which was cold, even by competitive swimming standards.

Brew shivered with a sympathetic chill when his brother hit the water.

"Did you see me?" Cody asked excitedly when he resurfaced. "Was that a cannonball?" And although it was more like a mad leap from the *Titanic*, I said, "Wow, you made quite a splash," which told him precisely what he needed to hear without lying to him. Then I turned to Brew, who still stood there with his hands in his pockets.

"Come on in; it's not that cold once you get used to it."

Cody, who had migrated down to the shallow end, called out to us. "Hey, watch me do a handstand!" He disappeared beneath the surface, produced some whitewater, then stood up again, arms spread in "ta-DA" position, seeking universal approval. "How was that?"

"Try it again," I told him. "It's easier if you keep your feet together."

While Cody occupied himself with underwater handstands, Brew strolled along the edge of the pool toward the shallow end, and I kept pace with him in the water.

"Are you coming in?" I asked.

"Maybe later," he said. "I just ate."

"Come on; it's not like you'll be swimming in a riptide," I told him. "If you get a cramp, I promise I'll save you."

Reluctantly he went to the steps, took off his shoes and socks, then waded gingerly into the shallowest part of the pool. The water didn't even come up to his waist. He wore a long-sleeved shirt, and it was already soaking up water at his waist and wrists.

"Aren't you going to take off your shirt?" I asked. Even before he responded, a spasmodic brain cell sparked out something Tennyson had said: *"Have you ever seen him with his shirt off?"* I mentally pinched the brain cell like a gnat and extinguished Tennyson's unwanted intrusion.

"Is it okay if I keep it on?" Brew said.

"Sure," I told him. "Did you know that in the old days, men's bathing suits included shirts?"

"I've heard that."

"And if a man took it off in a public place, he was thrown in jail."

"Really?"

"No, but I wouldn't put it past people in those days. The Victorian era was very uptight."

Apparently I didn't snuff out Tennyson's question fast enough, because it had acted like a pilot light, igniting my own curiosity. Why didn't Brew want to take off his shirt? It's not unusual for people to be shy about their bodies. They might feel their flesh tone is a little too pasty or their love handles are, shall we say, a little too "Michelin" in nature. I knew one boy who had a scar down the center of his chest from open-heart surgery as a baby. He hated taking off his shirt. Could it be something like that? Well, whatever Brewster's reason, I would deny my curiosity and respect his modesty. Truth be told, I found it charming.

"Did you see that handstand?" called Cody; and since I had actually seen feet flipping heavenward out of the corner of my eye, I said, "Much better. Keep practicing."

The water lily lady climbed out of the pool and smiled at me as she left, probably thinking *Ah! Young love,* as old people do. Now it was just the three of us in the pool.

Brew was leaning back against the pool edge, content just to stand there. I reached toward him, and he reluctantly came away from the wall. "It's best if you dunk all at once," I suggested. "Get the shock over with; otherwise you never get used to the water."

"I'm fine this way."

Now that he stood in slightly deeper water, the edge of his shirt grazed the surface, becoming darker as it soaked in pool water. "I'll race you to the far end," I suggested.

"No," he said. "I'm not very fast."

"So I'll just use my arms; I won't kick."

"No," he said, "I really don't want to."

I pulled him toward deeper water. "C'mon, it's only twenty-five yards."

"No!" he pulled his hand back from mine.

I looked at him, feeling like I had been slapped in the face, but then I realized I was the one who had pushed it. Then before either of us could say anything, Cody chimed in.

"Brew can't swim, but I can! One, two, three—GO!" And he took off toward the far end of the pool.

I looked at Brew, and he turned away. I could feel his humiliation like ripples in the water. "You really can't swim?"

He shook his head.

"Well, that's nothing to be ashamed of."

"Let's just drop it, okay?"

And suddenly I had an idea.

"I'll teach you to swim!" I said. Yes! It was absolutely perfect—and not just the answer to getting out of this awkward moment but also the ideal boy-girl bonding thing that becomes a musical montage in the movie version of our lives.

But before I could figure out where to start our first lesson, Brew said, "I'll be waiting in the stands." Then he turned to wade out of the pool.

"But it will be fun! I promise!" He didn't stop, so I reached for him and grabbed him, maybe a little too forcefully, because his feet slipped out from under him and he went down to his knees.

"Oops . . ."

We were still in water that was shallow enough so that it wasn't a problem, and he stood back up right away. But now his shirt had ridden up to his chest; and as he pulled it down, I got a brief glimpse of his body beneath the shirt. There was no taking back that glimpse. We both knew it.

"Did I win?" Cody shouted from the deep end. This time I didn't even answer him. I gave all my attention to Brewster.

"This was a bad idea," he said. "We should go."

I reached for him again—this time more gently—and I took his hand, holding it in a way that I never had before. The same way he had held my ankle the other day. Gently. Like it was something precious and fragile, even though his hand was so large compared to mine. "Don't go."

I could tell he just wanted to bolt. If he did, I wouldn't stop him. I had already pushed and pulled him in directions he didn't want to go. If he decided to leave, I resolved to let him. But he didn't.

I looked at his hand: His knuckles had scabs, but they were

softened by the water. I gently reached over and touched his shirt.

"Don't . . ."

"Please," I said. "Let me see."

"You don't want to see."

"Do you trust me?" I asked.

In his eyes, I could see the battle going on inside him. The desire to hide a terrible secret fighting with the desire to set it free.

He turned his back to me, and I thought he would leave then. But instead he stood, feet firm on the bottom of the pool, and said over his shoulder, "Okay. You can look if you want."

I began to lift up his shirt over his back, slowly, deliberately, like the rising of a curtain; and the scene it revealed was almost too much to bear.

His back was a battlefield.

Discolored flesh over old scars. I remembered stories about how they used to punish sailors by dragging them under a ship from one side to another across the rough, barnacle-encrusted hull. Keelhauling, they called it. Brewster looked like he had been keelhauled. Not once, but over and over. It wasn't just his back, either, because the marks extended around to his stomach and chest; and after I had pulled his shirt over his head and free from his arms, I could see a few marks on his arms as well. Although I couldn't see his legs underwater, I imagined they hadn't escaped the devastation either. I hadn't noticed it when he'd stepped into the pool; but then, I hadn't been looking.

I rarely feel true hatred toward anyone, but right then I despised the author of those wounds, glaringly written across his body like blunt hieroglyphics.

"Who did this to you?"

"No one," he said. Why did I know he would say that?

"You need to tell someone. The police, social services—anybody! Is it your uncle?"

"No! I told you it was nobody!"

"If you won't go to the police, I will!"

He turned to me, furious. "You said to trust you!"

"But you're lying to me! I have to trust you, too, and you're lying, because things like this just don't appear out of nowhere!"

"How do you know they don't?"

I took a deep breath and clenched my teeth. I didn't want any of the anger I was feeling to be directed at him. "If your uncle beats you, it will never stop if you don't do something about it."

Rather than answer me, he turned to Cody, who was now standing just a few yards away, chest-deep in the water.

"Cody, does Uncle Hoyt beat me?"

Cody seemed scared. He looked to Brew, then to me, then back to Brew again.

"It's okay," Brew said to him. "Tell her the truth."

Cody turned to me and shook his head. "No, Uncle Hoyt's afraid of Brewster."

"Has he ever hit me, even once?" Brew asked his brother.

Cody shook his head again. "No. Never."

Brew turned to me. "There. You see?"

Although I still didn't entirely believe it, there was an honesty in Brew's eyes. So I had to look for another explanation. The only other logical explanation was something I didn't want to consider, but I had to. And I had to ask.

"Then . . . do you do it to yourself?"

"No," he answered. "It's not that either."

I was relieved, but I still knew no more than before. "What then?"

He glanced at his brother, then around the pool, as if there might be someone nearby who'd hear what he was about to say. But we were all alone.

Finally he took a long look at me and shrugged, like it was nothing.

"It's a condition," he said. "That's all—just a condition. I bruise easily, and I've got thin skin. I always have. Sorry to disappoint you, but that's all it is. A condition."

I waited for more, but that's all he offered. I do know that people with low levels of iron in their blood tend to bruise easily, but it just didn't ring true. "You mean . . . like anemia?"

He nodded. I could sense immense sorrow in that nod. "Something like that."

17) CONUNDRUM

Things were more strained than usual at dinner that night, but it could just have been that my senses were on high alert. Things around me had become confusing; I didn't know if I could trust my own perceptions anymore, and my thoughts were preoccupied with Brewster.

My parents, who used to be so much more observant, had absolutely no clue that anything was troubling me. Their own personal universes had developed a shell so thick, I don't think anything was getting through from the outside.

"Are you done, Brontë?" Mom asked, reaching for my dinner plate, not even noticing that I hadn't eaten a single thing. Carbs, protein, fiber—it all just sat there, as appetizing as plastic to me.

"I'm done," I told her. She took away my plate and scraped my dinner into the disposal. I guess if I wasn't so focused on

Brew, I might have realized how "off" things were, how our whole family was on the verge of a landslide. Right then I wasn't seeing anything, though.

But Tennyson was. He was the one who noticed that Mom and Dad didn't say a word to each other all evening—how Dad just ate in silence. Tennyson even noticed my lack of appetite.

"Starvation diet?" he asked.

"Maybe I'm just not hungry," I said. "Did you think of that?"

"I guess it's contagious," he said. Only then did I realize he hadn't eaten much either. In fact, all he had eaten were his vegetables.

"Since when are you a vegetarian?" I asked.

He looked at me, taking great offense. "Just because I don't feel like eating meat lately doesn't make me a vegetarian. I'm not a vegetarian, okay?" Then he stormed away from the table.

After dinner I tried to do my homework, but I simply couldn't focus. I knew why. I had avoided talking to Tennyson about Brewster, but I couldn't put it off any longer. He was, unfortunately, the only one I could talk to.

I found him in the family room, watching basketball. He was slouching in the man-eating sofa—the one that, when we were kids, we could sink into and practically disappear. It looked like Tennyson was still trying to do that; but the older we get, the harder that is.

"I'm sorry," I said. "I didn't mean to call you a vegetarian."

"Apology accepted," he said without looking at me. And when I didn't leave, he said, "You wanna watch the game?"

I sat beside him and let the sofa pull me in. We watched the game for a few minutes, and finally I said:

"I saw it."

He turned to me, only half interested. "Saw what?"

"His back," I told him. "He took off his shirt, and I saw his back. And it's not just on his back; it's all over."

Tennyson shifted forward out of the folds of the man-eating sofa and raised the remote, turning off the TV, and gave me his full attention. I was grateful that this was more important to him than the game.

"So, what do you think?" he asked. "Do you think it's his uncle?"

Well, I know what I thought, but Brewster swore up and down that it wasn't true. "I don't know," I told my brother. "He's a conundrum—and there's still a piece missing from the puzzle." Whatever that piece was, there was a part of me telling me not to get involved—that it was too much to handle. That you shouldn't go out on a limb unless you're absolutely sure the limb can support your weight.

But a stronger part of me wanted to know everything about Brewster Rawlins and become a part of his story, no matter how harsh that story was.

Tennyson opened his mouth to speak again, but I didn't let him.

"I know what you're going to say. You're going to say 'I told you so,' then you're going to look at me with that smug expression you get whenever you're accidentally right."

Then Tennyson did something he rarely does. He caught me by surprise.

"No," he said, "I think you should keep seeing him."

I tried to read the expression on his face, but with the TV turned off and only dim lights in the room, I couldn't. "Are you being sarcastic?" I asked. "Because it's not funny."

"No," said Tennyson. "I mean it. If you care about him, then you should keep on seeing him. Do you care about him?"

I didn't answer right away. I'll admit that Brewster had started as a project, but he had quickly become more than that. The question wasn't whether or not I cared about him; the question was, how much? I'm glad Tennyson didn't ask *that*, because then I'd have to ask myself; and I already knew the answer. I cared far more than was safe.

"Yes," I told Tennyson simply. "I do care about him."

Tennyson nodded and, without an ounce of judgment, said, "Good. Because he probably needs you. And I think you're going to need him, too."

I didn't quite know what he meant by that last part, but I

was still processing the fact that Tennyson felt this was good.

"I thought you hated him. . . ."

"I did," Tennyson admitted, "but if I wanted to keep hating him, I needed a good reason; and I couldn't find one."

This was not the Tennyson I knew. It's amazing how people can surprise you. Even brothers. "So, now you're friends?"

"I wouldn't go *that* far." Then Tennyson lifted his hand and made a fist. I thought he was making a point; but no, he just studied his knuckles with a creepy kind of intensity. "Tell me something, Brontë; by any chance did you hurt your foot last week?"

It threw me because I didn't expect him to know about that. How does he find out these things? "Yes," I said. "I mean, no. I mean, I thought I sprained my ankle, but I didn't."

"And the Bruiser was with you?"

"Were you spying on us again?"

"No, I just had a hunch."

"So, then, he told you about it?"

"Nope." And then he added with a grin, "Maybe I'm just a mind reader."

Now this was more like the Tennyson I knew. "The only thing supernatural about you, Tennyson, is your body odor."

He laughed at that. It eased the tension, but only a little. Then he got serious again. "Just promise me that you'll stay away from his house and from his uncle . . . and if things start to get weird, you'll tell me."

"What do you mean by *weird*?"

"Just promise," he said.

"Okay, fine. I promise."

Then Tennyson leaned back into the man-eating sofa and turned on the TV, signaling the end of the conversation.

I left feeling more unsettled than before. It was easier to deal with Tennyson when he was fighting me; but having him on my side was frightening, because now I didn't know who the enemy was.

18) PERIPHERALLY

In horse racing they put these slats on either side of the horse's head, blocking the creature's peripheral vision. They're called blinders. They don't actually blind the horse, but they allow the horse to see only what's right in front of it; otherwise it might freak out and lose the race.

People live with blinders too; but ours are invisible, and much more sophisticated. Most of the time we don't even know they're there. Maybe we need them, though, because if we took in everything all at once, we'd lose our minds. Or worse, our souls. We'd see, we'd hear, we'd *feel* so deeply that we might never resurface.

So we make decisions and base our lives on those decisions, never realizing we're only seeing one-tenth of the whole. Then we cling to our narrow conclusions like our lives depend on it.

Remember how they imprisoned Galileo for insisting the earth revolved around the sun? You can call those people ignorant, but it was more than mere ignorance. They had a lot to lose if they took off their blinders. Can you imagine how terrifying it must be to suddenly realize that everything you believe about the nature of the universe is wrong? Most people don't realize how terrifying that is until *their* world is the one being threatened.

My world always revolved around our nuclear family. Mom, Dad, Tennyson, and me. It was an atom that might ionize once in a while, erratically spewing electrons here and there; but in spite of that, I always believed it was fundamentally stable. No one expects nuclear fission within the loving bonds of one's own family.

My blinders didn't allow me to see it coming.

19) GASTRONOMY

I promised Tennyson I wouldn't go to Brewster's house, but that didn't mean I couldn't invite him to ours.

It was Friday, and I was already cooking dinner when Mom came home from the university. I had told her and Dad that tonight was the night Brew was coming; but I still couldn't take the chance that Mom would forget and have to order fast food, or worse, pull out frozen burritos and try to pass them off as homemade. So I skipped Friday's swim practice and got dinner going myself, thank you very much.

Sure enough, Mom's mind was beyond elsewhere when she got home, so I had definitely made the right call. "Brewster will be coming at six," I told her. "Just in time for dinner. Please, *please*, don't bring out my baby pictures, or ask him about his philosophy of life the way you did with Max."

Mom nodded, then said, "I'm sorry, honey, what was that?" like she was somewhere in deep space, where sound waves couldn't travel. It drove me crazy that I had to repeat myself, and I still don't know whether she heard.

If it weren't for my blinders, I might have wondered about the bigger picture, but right then and there it was all about me.

"Please *try* to make him feel at home. Please *try* not to scare him away."

"Did your father call?" Mom asked with an emptiness in her voice that I misread as exhaustion.

"I don't know," I told her. "I've been out buying groceries."

Tennyson arrived a bit later, all sweaty from lacrosse.

"Shower!" I ordered. "Brewster's coming over for dinner."

He looked worried and said to me quietly, "I don't think this is a good night."

"When is it ever?"

"No," he said just as quietly. "There's something wrong. Something going on. I could tell this morning at breakfast; didn't you notice the way Mom and Dad were?"

"No."

"It's like . . . it's like someone died and they haven't told us yet. Anyway, whatever it is—"

"Whatever it is," I said stridently, "it's going to have to wait until after dinner. I've been planning this for a week, dinner is in the oven, and it's too late to call it off."

He gave no further argument and went off to shower.

When Dad came home, he opened a bottle of wine, which wasn't unusual. He'd usually have a glass as he watched the news, and maybe one with dinner if the wine was one that complemented the meal—but never more than that. Tonight he guzzled the first glass with the wine bottle still in his hand and poured a second. I thought about what Tennyson had said but decided that whatever was wrong, a hearty, home-cooked meal would soothe it.

"Dad, save the second glass for dinner," I told him. "Merlot goes well with what I'm making."

"You?"

"Yes, me. Brewster's coming for dinner, remember?"

"Oh. Right."

Brewster arrived just as I finished setting the table. "Am I too early?" he asked.

"Right on time," I told him. "You look great." He was dressed in slacks and a button-down shirt that was a little bit small on him; but that was his own personal style, and I'd come to appreciate it. His wavy hair was so well-groomed, he was hardly recognizable. I practically wanted to put him up as the centerpiece of the table and present him proudly to my parents; but instead I just made introductions, and they all shook hands.

Then, when everyone was seated, I brought the platter to the table. "*Voilà*," I said. "*Bon appétit*." And I unveiled my gastronomical masterpiece.

Tennyson and Brew just stared at it like it had come from Mars.

"What is that?" Tennyson asked.

"It's a tri-tip roast," I said.

Tennyson looked like he might become physically ill. "Where'd you get it?" he asked.

"The store. Where else?"

"I'll pass."

"What do you mean, you'll pass? You can't pass! I was cooking all afternoon!"

Tennyson turned to Brew, and Brew grinned. "Still not eating meat?"

"I'll eat it when I'm good and ready," said Tennyson.

The fact that the two of them had some secret that I wasn't aware of really bothered me. "Are you going to tell me what this is all about?"

"Not while we're eating," said Tennyson, and he loaded his plate with asparagus, announcing that it didn't make him a vegetarian.

"It's a lovely dinner, Brontë," said Mom; but instead of eating, she got up to clean the pots and pans that I had cooked with, refusing to sit down again.

Dad said nothing about the meal, or about anything else. He served himself and picked at the food on his plate, glaring down with an intensity that was both cold and hot at the same time, like he had a vendetta against the roast and hated each and every vicious spear of asparagus before him.

The silence around the table was awful and simply had to be broken, but no one was willing to do it but me.

"It's not usually like this," I told Brew. "That is to say, it's not really this quiet. Usually we have conversations—especially when we have guests. Right?"

Finally Dad took the hint. "So, exactly how long have you known each other?" he asked, but his tone was strangely bitter.

"We started going out three weeks ago, if that's what you mean," Brew said. "But we've known each other since elementary school. Or at least known *of* each other."

Dad shoved a piece of meat into his mouth and spoke with his mouth full. "Glad to hear it," he said as he cut another piece of meat. "You have my blessing," he said to me. "*Via con Dios.*"

It was the most mad-bizarre thing I'd ever heard my father say. I turned to see Mom's reaction, but she was still busy washing the pots and pans, keeping her back to the rest of us.

Finally I lost it. *"What's wrong with you?"* I shouted to Mom and Dad.

No answer for a while. Then Dad said, "Nothing's wrong, Brontë. I'm just worried about your mother. She's putting so much effort into that 'Monday night class' she teaches, I'm concerned for her health." He glared at her back like it was an accusation. Suddenly I realized that it was.

For a brief moment I met Brew's eyes, and there was panic in them. I could see the way he held his utensils tightly in his hands, as if he'd have to use them as weapons at any moment. I turned to Tennyson, whose hands were out, palms down on the table; he was looking at his plate as if he were silently saying grace. *No, that's not it,* I realized. *My brother's bracing himself. Bracing himself for what?*

And suddenly my blinders fell away, letting the big picture invade my mind in all of its terrible glory.

20) OBLIVIOUS

Enola Gay is the name of the plane that dropped the atomic bomb on Hiroshima and, three days later, on Nagasaki. It flew so high that when it released a bomb, it took one minute and forty-three seconds for the bomb to reach the ground. Actually, I made that part up; but you know what? I don't care. I'm sure it's close.

I wonder what the crewmen were thinking during that time between the act and the result. Were they regretful? Were they frightened? Exhilarated? Numb? Or were they just thinking about getting home to their families?

The thing is, once a bomb begins to fall the deed is done. All you can do is watch helplessly, waiting for the blinding flash.

I never saw it coming, but Tennyson did. I think he watched for the whole minute forty-three. It must have torn him apart inside to know that Mom and Dad were about to go thermo-nuclear, and also know that he could do nothing to stop it. All he could do was brace himself. He tried to warn me, but I was too oblivious to duck and cover.

Maybe I was the lucky one, because by the time I saw it, the bomb was about to strike the hardpan earth, so I never knew what hit me. And Brew? Well, he was the innocent bystander caught in precisely the wrong place at precisely the wrong time.

21) DETONATION

"How about it, Lisa?" Dad taunted from his place at the table. "Care to share the gist of your Monday night class? Or is it not suitable for children?"

Mom slammed down one of the pots in the sink. "Stop it, Daniel," she said. "Now is not the time."

"Of course it's not," Dad said. "But why should that ever make a difference?"

And then Dad turned to the three of us—me, Brew, and Tennyson—like we were a tribunal of Supreme Court justices. "Let me tell you about life," he said. "Life is all about revenge. Getting back at the other guy at all costs; isn't that right, Lisa? Why don't you tell everyone about your 'class'?"

"I'm not talking about this!" But she finally turned to face him, proving that yes, she *was* talking about this.

"Say it, Lisa. I need to hear you say it. I need to hear it from *you*."

"Dad!" shouted Tennyson. "Stop it! Leave her alone!"

But Dad put up his hand with such authority, Tennyson backed down. He's the only person Tennyson will back down from.

Dad looked at Mom for a moment more, both with matching gazes of accusation and rage . . . and then it was over. Dad crumbled. He buried his head in his hands and burst into tears that went on and on with no sign of stopping.

I turned to my mother, desperately hoping she could say something to fix this. "Mom?" I said. "What's going on? What's Dad talking about?"

Her shoulders went slack; and before her own emotions could choke out her voice, she said, "There *is* no Monday night class, Brontë."

That's when Brewster bolted. He stood up so quickly that he nearly knocked over the dinner table and made a beeline for the door—and since it was easier to go after him than it was to stand there and face my crumbling, dissolving parents, I followed him.

"Brew! Wait!"

He didn't turn back to me until he was safely across the threshold of our front door. "I shouldn't even be here," he said. "My uncle's at work, my brother's home alone—"

"I'll come with you. . . ." I reached for him, but he pushed my arms away.

"I can't *do* this!" He was furious. He was terrified. "You don't understand! I can't care about them. I can't care about *you*!"

"What?"

He backed away, but he held me in his horrible, deep, draining eyes. "That's right. I don't care about you. It's over. I don't care about you at all." Then he turned and took off like a thief, disappearing down the street and into the windy night.

22) REFLEXIVELY

There would be no looking back on this and laughing. That's what people always say, isn't it? "Someday you'll look back on this and laugh." Easy for them to say. I hope they choke on their own advice.

Standing at the open door was like standing at the edge of the earth. I felt myself leaning forward into the April wind, wishing I could just jump—or better yet, just slip out of my body and drift away, leaving all the pain of the evening far behind.

The thing was, if I had found a way to escape—even for just a little while—I knew the pain would be there waiting for me when I got back.

But for now I was shell-shocked. It wasn't quite escape, but it would have to do.

"Fine," I said to the stupid, soulless wind, and went inside.

No one was in the kitchen when I returned, and I happily entertained the fantasy that Mom and Dad had been instantly vaporized by their own middle-aged angst and had taken Tennyson along with them. An evil thought, I know; but I was feeling evil down to the core right then—and perfectly entitled to the feeling.

I could hear the TV in the family room. Probably Tennyson. And I heard movement upstairs—Mom or Dad, but not both, because by now they would have retreated to their separate corners of the ring, probably finding the two farthest points in the house to lick their wounds.

And there in front of me were the ruins of the evening on our best china. The waste products of a dinner gone wrong.

I found myself cleaning up, because it was easier to do something simple like clearing the table than to analyze which level of hell I now resided in.

I wasn't being as attentive as I should have been, however, because as I reached to grab the serving platter, my thumb sliced across the sharp edge of the carving knife. I reflexively drew back my hand, but it was too late; there was a half-inch gash on my palm, near the base of my left thumb, and it was already oozing blood.

"Crap!"

I grabbed it with my other hand and tried to stem the flow of blood, but it didn't help. Blood dribbled in little vermillion drops all over the forsaken roast, blending in with the drippings.

And that's when I started to cry.

Of all the stupid things. Never mind that my boyfriend just abandoned me and my family just auto-destructed—there I was, crying about that stupid, freaking roast.

"Brontë?" Tennyson stood in the doorway watching me bleed onto dinner. "What happened?"

I grabbed a cloth napkin from an untouched table setting, pressed it to my bleeding hand, and to my own embarrassment found myself whimpering like a child. "It's all ruined, Tennyson," I said. "Everything."

"C'mon," he said; and he grabbed my elbow, pulling me toward the bathroom.

He searched for Band-Aids in the medicine chest while I washed the wound, watching the pink water flow down the drain.

"Apply pressure," he said.

"I know how to stop bleeding!" I snapped. "I took lifesaving, for God's sake!"

"Okay, okay, I'm just trying to help."

I cleaned it with peroxide, and he held out a Band-Aid. "At least let me help you put this on," Tennyson said. "You can't do it with one hand."

So I held out my hand and let him stretch the bandage across the wound, smoothing out the adhesive strip.

"There," he said. "I don't think you'll need stitches."

I took a deep breath. "Thank you, Tennyson."

"No problem."

As much as we fought, I can't deny that at times like this, there's a closeness between us that I've always been grateful for.

We didn't leave the bathroom. Instead, he closed the door and sat on the toilet lid while I stretched out in the dry bathtub. It wasn't the most comfortable place for a sibling summit meeting, but there's something comforting about the tight privacy of a family bathroom. Does that sound weird? I don't care.

I told him all about how Brewster bailed.

He told me about the times he'd picked up the phone only to be hung up on—and the time he'd overheard Mom talking to someone, saying things she should be saying to no one but Dad.

"Mom has a boyfriend," Tennyson said.

So there it was, out in the open. No hints, just the plain, raw fact.

"It's because of what Dad did last year, isn't it?"

"Maybe," said Tennyson. "Maybe not. Maybe it would have happened anyway."

Mom and Dad had tried to keep it hidden last year, but Tennyson and I knew what Dad had done. We had been furious about it, because fathers are not supposed to have girlfriends—even if it's only for a short time. Even if it's only one time. They're not supposed to, but sometimes they do.

Fact of life. I don't know the statistics. Maybe I should look them up.

So it happened, and Dad had been left with a choice. He could give her up, whoever she was, and then move heaven and earth to make things right with Mom. Or he could end the marriage. He'd chosen Mom—and Tennyson and I saw how he tried to make it up, not just to Mom, but to all of us. I guess that had been enough for us to forgive him—at least in part. I had thought it was the same with Mom. I never understood the depth of the wound.

All at once, I found my thoughts ricocheting to Brewster. As much as it hurt to think of him, it was easier than thinking about my parents. It was easier to condemn him for what he had done; and the more I thought about it, the angrier I got. I had reached out to save him from whatever terrible things were going on in his world; but when something went seriously wrong in mine, he didn't just walk away, he ran.

"He just washed his hands of us," I mumbled. "He washed his hands of *me*."

"Did you expect him to be a model of mental stability?" Tennyson asked. "You don't get a reputation as the resident creepy dude for nothing."

Still, that wasn't an excuse. There was no excuse for the way he behaved. If I could be sure of nothing else that evening, I could be sure of that.

"I hate him," I said, and at the moment I meant it with all my heart. "I hate him."

Beyond the bathroom wall, we heard the garage door grind open and a car started. Someone drove away. I didn't know whether it was Mom or Dad. I didn't want to find out.

"So, what happens now?" Tennyson asked. It surprised me, because between the two of us, he was always the one who pretended to have the answer.

"It'll get worse before it gets better," I said.

"The D word?"

"The S word first," I pointed out. I couldn't imagine our parents separating. Who would move out, Mom or Dad? Who would we live with? Did we get to choose? How could we possibly choose?

Tennyson and I didn't talk anymore, because there was nothing left to say; but we didn't leave the bathroom either, because this was, at least for the time being, our only place of safety. So we sat there in silence, wishing there was some way to sleep through whatever was to come. Wishing there was someone who could come and magically take away all the pain.

23) TRANSFERENCE

It's strange how we always want other people to feel what we feel. It must be a basic human drive. Misery loves company, right? Or when you see a movie that you love, don't you want to drag all your friends to see it as well? Because it's only good the second time if it's the first time for somebody else—as if their experience somehow resonates inside of you. The power of shared experiences. Maybe it's a way to remind ourselves that on some level we're all connected.

By morning we knew that it was Mom who had left, and she hadn't come home. Dad made us breakfast: credible pancakes, although the blackened evidence of his first batch was buried in the trash.

"She'll be back when you get home," Dad told us. He seemed way too confident about that, which made me think that he wasn't confident about it at all.

As we walked to school, I couldn't stop thinking about how furious I still was with Brew—how I wanted to make him feel everything I had felt last night: the helplessness of watching my family detonate and the soul-searing feeling of being abandoned in the midst of it, the way he had done to me. I wanted to take everything I was feeling, put it into a cannon, then aim it at him.

I knew I'd see Brew in school that day, and what bothered me most was that I didn't know what I'd do when I saw him. It was terrifying not to have a perfect and clear-cut course of action. I knew exactly when I would see him, too. His locker was just outside of my second-period class. Usually we looked forward to seeing each other then, even if it was just to say hello. Now I dreaded it.

I suppose he could've made a point of avoiding his locker, but he didn't. And I suppose I could have slipped in through the classroom's back door, but I didn't do that either—because as much as I was dreading it, I knew it had to happen.

He was standing right there as I approached the classroom. He didn't look at me. He just stared into his locker, moving around books.

"Brewster?"

He turned to me and I found my arm swinging even before I was conscious of the motion. I guess swimming made me stronger than I realized, because I slapped him so hard, his head snapped to the side, hitting his locker, which rang out like a bell. It was all I could do to keep myself from pounding on his chest. All of that fury I was feeling needed a way out.

Around us, other kids saw what was going on. Some gave us a wide berth, others laughed, and that only made me angrier. And then Brewster said:

"Is that it? Because I have to get to class."

"No!" I shouted, "that's not it!" and I pushed him. I realized I was doing the bully thing that my brother was famous for, but at the moment I didn't care. The push didn't do much anyway—Brew had so much inertia, he didn't even move when I pushed him. Instead, I ended up stumbling backward.

"There are things you don't know," he said.

"You think you can hide behind that?" I shouted. "That's no excuse! What you did last night . . . what you *said*—"

"I lied."

That caught me off guard and I hesitated, trying to figure out just what he had lied about. He'd said he didn't care about me, or about any of us. Was he lying about that? Did he care after all? Did I want him to?

The tardy bell rang. We were alone in the hallway now. I was about to turn and storm into class when I felt something warm and wet on my hand. It was blood.

"Oh no!" It didn't take a genius to figure out I had opened the gash on my hand again. The Band-Aid, which was already loose, was now too wet to hold its grip. It slipped off; and when I brushed away the blood, I had trouble relocating the exact spot of the wound. As it turns out, the blood wasn't coming from my cut at all.

"It's not you; it's me," Brew said, which is one of the lines guys use when they break up with you; but that wasn't the case here. It *was* him. He was the one bleeding.

He pursed his lips. "Not good," he said. "Not good at all."

My anger didn't exactly go away at that instant, but it did hop into the backseat. "I must have cut you with my watch," I said, although I couldn't imagine anything sharp enough on my watch to draw that much blood. "We've got to get you to the nurse."

As Brew pressed on the wound to staunch the bleeding at the base of his thumb, I reached into my backpack and found a little pocket-pack of tissues. I pressed the whole pack to his hand and hurried with him down the hall.

"I can do it myself," he said.

"I don't care," I told him.

We pushed through the door of the nurse's office, where some boy I didn't know looked up at me with feverish eyes and a God-help-me expression, like he thought he might die at any moment.

"Get in line," he said.

"I don't think so." I shoved past him toward the nurse. By now the whole tissue pack on Brew's hand was soaked through with blood, and the moment the nurse saw it, she went into triage mode. She quickly assessed the damage and began to clean the gash with gauze and antiseptic.

"What happened?"

"I got cut on my locker door," Brew said.

Is that what happened? I thought. *But he wasn't even touching his locker.*

"It looks worse than it is," the nurse said once the wound had been cleaned. "You probably won't even need stitches." She talked about tetanus shots and gave him a thick piece of gauze. "Keep pressure on it." Then she turned to me and my bloody fingers. "And you need to clean yourself up. There's a sink over there. Wash all the way to your elbows. Do it twice." She told Brew she'd be back to dress the wound, then went to deal with the plague-ridden boy by the door.

I went to the sink, crisis resolved, except, of course, for one minor thing:

The wound was gone from my hand.

It hadn't healed—it was gone, like it had never been there at all. I kept washing my hands, certain I had just missed it and that it would reappear once I washed away the lather, but no. The cut was nowhere to be found.

I could feel something tugging on the edge of my awareness. Something both frightening and wonderful. I was at the barrier of some unknown place. Even as I stood there I could feel myself crossing over that line.

When I turned to Brew, he was watching me.

"You didn't cut yourself on a locker, did you?" I asked.

He shook his head. I sat beside him, not quite ready to believe what had happened.

"Let me see it."

He raised the gauze. The wound had clotted; the blood had stopped flowing. I could see the wound clearly now. It was my wound. Same size, same place. Only now it was on *his* hand.

"Do you understand now?" he asked gently.

But how could I understand? This wasn't an answer; it was a question—and one I didn't even know how to ask. All I could say was "How?"

"I don't know," he said. "It just happens."

"Always? With everyone?"

"No," he said. "Not everyone." The wound had begun to ooze again, so he pressed the gauze to it. "But if I care about someone . . ."

He didn't have to finish the thought, because it was there in his eyes. The reason why he ran—why he lied. People thought Brewster Rawlins was a dark unknown, a black hole best kept away from. Well, maybe he was, but what people don't realize is that black holes generate an amazing amount of light. The problem is, their gravity is so great, the light can't escape—it just gets pulled in along with everything else.

If he took away the sprains, cuts, and bruises of everyone he cared about, no wonder he'd rather be alone. How could

I blame him for running last night as he tried to escape his own gravity?

I could feel my anger and turmoil draining away now that I had at least a part of the puzzle. The brooding expression on Brew's face truly was inscrutable, so it was impossible to know what he was feeling; but I knew what *I* was feeling. It flowed in to fill the void once my anger was gone. As unexpected as the slap, I found myself kissing him; and although I heard the nurse protesting from across the room, her voice sounded miles away. I was caught in a gravity far greater than hers.

"I love you, Brew."

"No you don't," he said.

"Just shut up and take it," I told him.

He smiled. "Okay."

He didn't have to tell me that he felt the same, because I already knew. The evidence was there on the palm of his hand.

BREWSTER

24) INJURIOUS

I saw the weak hearts of my classmates shredded by
      conformity, bloated and numb, as they iced the
      wounds of acceptance in the primordial gym, hoping
      to heal themselves into popularity,
Who have devolved into Play-Doh pumped through a
      sleazy suburban press, stamped in identical molds,
      all bearing chunks of bleak ice, comet-cold in their
      chests,
Who look down their surgically set noses at me, the boy
      most likely to die by lethal injection with no crime
      beyond the refusal to permit their swollen, shredded
      cardiac chill to fill my heart as well,
Yet out of this frigid pool of judgment stepped Brontë,
      untainted by the cold, radiating warmth in a
      rhythmic pulse through her veins, echoing now in
      mine, just as the slice across her palm is now my

burden, taken by accident, yet held with purposeful
        triumph,
As I now reach to double-check the unreliable lock on my
        bathroom door, which gives no privacy, least of all
        from Uncle Hoyt, who, in fits of paranoia, must
        know everything, *everything* that goes on beneath his
        termite-ridden, shingle-shedding roof,
Where I now carefully peel the bandage from my hand,
        revealing shades of brown and red, flesh damaged
        and bruised, hoping to redress the wound before my
        uncle can find out, the wound that I have no idea
        how Brontë got, for in my fuzz-brained love haze, I
        forgot to question,
Which will heal without mystery or magic at the normal
        pace of life — in a week, two weeks, three — like the
        raw-knuckle scabs of her brother, now mine, too,
        like the bruises, breaks, and scrapes, the scars of a
        lifelong battle that defines me,
Like the fresh wound that cannot be concealed as my
        uncle swings open the maliciously disloyal
        bathroom door, and getting a healthy look at the
        fresh red line sliced across the heel of my hand,
        knowing from my unmet gaze that I'm holding
        a secret, which gives him permission to hold me
        hostage.

"Get that cut today, did you?"
"Yes."
"Didja take it from Cody?"
"No."
"That boy'd cut his head off with safety scissors."
"I didn't take it from Cody; it happened at school."

My uncle knows about the things I can do—the pain that I
  take—and knowing makes him still crazier and more
  protective, but of himself, not of me.
I muffle the screaming wound with a white gauze square;
  but nervous, tense, I press too hard and wince, a
  small twitch almost imperceptible, and he's looking
  at me with searing intensity, seeing all.

"Hurt?"
"No."
"You're lying."
"It's nothing."
"It don't look like nothing."
"It'll heal."
"You gonna tell me how you got it?"

He, with zero trust, zero tolerance, zeroes in on my eyes that
  once knew only how to betray me but lately have
  learned the wicked wartime trick of holding secrets in

a darker place and coding them to a cipher my uncle
isn't clever enough to crack.

"I told you it's nothing. Some girl in the hallway."
"Some girl?"
*"Coulda been something sharp on her backpack; I don't
know."*
"And you're saying I should believe that?"
"I'm saying you should take your dump and let me be."

And, as I leave the bathroom, my uncle hurls a warning
scowl to remind me that mouthing off will buy me a
world of punishment, but not today, because it's not
worth his time, then he closes the door to take the
call of nature, leaving me to stride, giddy with relief,
down the hall and into the room I share with my
brother,
Where Cody plays with plastic army men, and he, the
general of a pigsty battlefront, glances at my
bandaged hand but asks no questions, sibling-smart
in his willful ignorance, knowing he can't know,
because eight-year-olds don't just tell secrets, they
sing them on every unwanted wavelength, and since
Cody's mouth betrays him even more often than my
eyes betray me, he doesn't ask, because he knows he
can't sing to our uncle the things I haven't told him,

So the wound remains secure as I lie on my bed, like a
        blood oath aching a sweet reminder of the secret I
        share with Brontë, this moment marking the first
        time I've seen my gift as a wonder and not a curse,
For standing between Cody and his pain is my obligation,
        and standing between my uncle and his pain is my
        rent, but the pain I coax from Brontë is my joy.

25) EPIC

I will not give in
To an interrogation
Even from Brontë

On a day in the park where wind-torn clouds sweep a
      frenetic sky in vivid Van Gogh strokes, while Brontë
      and I read Homer on the grass, studying for an epic
      exam of cyclopean proportions, I will not give in to
      the interrogation,
As Cody jumps from a tree, oblivious to the strain he puts
      on my shins, then climbs again recklessly, no
      thought of consequences, his survival skills a casualty
      of his painless existence, I will not give in to the
      interrogation,

While Brontë leans into my lap, and I read *The Odyssey* aloud, feeling her need to know grow stronger the longer I avoid it, until she notices that I'm reciting the book entirely from memory, and she finds the first question to begin the barrage—but just as Odysseus resists the sirens, I will not give in to the interrogation.

"You memorized The Odyssey*?"*
"So what? Homer did it, and I'm not even blind."
"The whole thing?"
"Only the parts I've read."
"That's amazing, Brew."
"It's just something I do."
"Like the healing?"
"It's not healing; it's stealing."
"Excuse me?"
"The pain doesn't leave; it just jumps to me."
"How do you explain that?"
"I don't."

As the sun hides behind the shearing clouds, the temperature plunges and frustrated mothers race to their children, coats at the ready to battle the schizophrenic day, and Brontë ignores the breeze, knowing the sun will strobe on again in a moment;

yet if she's cold she does not care, because she's
        begun the inquisition,
And I wonder if her need to know is stronger than my need
        to remain unexposed.

> *"How did it start?*
> *Do you choose who you heal?*
> *How do you choose?*
> *Who do you choose?*
> *Does anyone know?*
> *How does it work?*
> *Do you have to be touching?*
> *Why won't you answer?*
> *Aren't you listening?*
> *Brew?"*

Even as I offer Brontë nothing but silence, her hand
        ventures beneath my shirt, roaming my back to make
        a gentle accounting of my wounds—asking me if it
        hurts, telling her that it does, just a little—then her
        hand moves around to my chest, and just as I realize
        she's not feeling wounds anymore, she tickles my
        neck, giggles, and pulls back her hand, and I think
        how different this is—how I've never been teased,
        at least not like this, not the way a girl teases her
        boyfriend,

And the raw power of that thought makes me surrender,
giving in to the interrogation, willfully spilling forth
things I've never told a soul.

"For as long as I can remember I've stolen,
Ripping all the hurts from the people I love,
And from no one else.
I don't choose it,
I don't want it,
But because they found a place in my heart
I steal their pain as soon as I'm near them,
And all because I got caught caring.
But those others,
ALL the others,
Dripping their disapproval like summer sweat,
They're on the outside,
And I will never let them in.
Never.
Let them keep their broken bones,
Shed their own blood,
I hate them.
I have to hate them, don't you see?
Because what if I didn't?
What if I suddenly started to care?
And their friends became my friends,
And every ache and pain,

Every last bit of damage,
Drained from them to me,
Until I was nothing but fractures and sprains,
Cuts and concussions,
But as long as I keep them on the right side of resentment,
Despising them all,
I'm safe."

Listening keenly, passing no judgment, Brontë takes it all in,
then leaning close, she kisses my ear, healing me in
a way she will never understand, and she whispers,
"But you did choose to care about Tennyson and me.
You let us in, Brew."
So I nod and whisper back: "Promise you'll close the door
behind you."

26) ENUMERATION

Here are the ten things
I will never tell Brontë
Or anyone else:

1) My father could be one of five men I've met,
   And after having met them,
   I don't want to know.

2) Cody's only my half brother, but he doesn't know it.
   I once knew his father, but not his last name,
   Or where to find him.

3) Men were constantly falling in love with my mother,
   They thought she took away their innermost pain.

But that was actually me.

4) We once joined a cult that eventually changed its name
   To The Sentinels of Brewster.
   I don't want to talk about it.

5) My mother developed ovarian cancer.
   But I couldn't take it away;
   I have no ovaries.

6) She left us with Uncle Hoyt when she first got sick;
   She knew if it spread to other organs,
   I would get it, too.

7) She called me every day until she died.
   I still talk to her once in a while.
   When no one's listening.

8) Someday I want the government to find me,
   And pay me millions of dollars
   To sit near the president.

9) Someday I want to be on a Wheaties box,
   Or at least on the cover
   Of *TIME* magazine.

10) Someday I want to wake up and be normal.
Just for a little while.
Or forever.

27) ORIFICE

With neck hairs standing on end, secret panic tripping in my
      brain, I cross into the petri dish of despair, the chasm
      of chaos, the school cafeteria,
Where larval troglodytes of blue and white collar breeds
      practice the vicious social skills of peacock preening
      and primate posturing amid the satanic smell of
      institutional ravioli,
When I reluctantly join the line for food, I avoid all eyes
      but notice, across the cafeteria, Tennyson and his
      girlfriend, Katrina,
Who cling to each other like statically charged particles, and
      I wonder if Brontë might cling to me in the same
      way, even while under the judgmental glare of the
      hormonal high school petting zoo, if she didn't avoid
      the cafeteria on principle,

When a hairless ape named Ozzy O'Dell forces his way in
front of me as if I'm nothing more than a piece of
soy-stretched meat lurking in the ravioli and calls me
the nickname he would much rather call the special
ed kids, if he could get away with it.

"Hey, Short-bus, make some room."
"No. The end of the line's back there."
"I don't think so—we're in a hurry."
"So am I."
"For what? Freak practice?"

While he laughs at his own idiotic joke, I think how, in the
past, I would just let it go, but meeting Brontë has
changed me, and I'm boldly standing up for myself
in places that used to give me vertigo, so as the lazy-
eyed lunch lady hands Ozzy a plate of ravioli, I tell
him how shaving his head for swim team was not
a good idea, because it emphasizes how small his
brain is, the same way his Speedo emphasizes how
small other things are,
Which makes his friends laugh at him instead of at me, and
Ozzy laughs, too, telling me it's so funny I deserve
to get my ravioli first, because I've earned it, then
he hands over his plate full of the slithery, sluglike
pasta pockets, and I'm confused enough to think that

maybe he's sincere, because I don't know the rules of
the game,

When he rests his finger on the edge of my tray, not
forcefully enough for the lazy-eyed lunch lady to
notice but enough to shift the balance and flip the
whole tray, turning the ravioli into projectile pasta,
splattering every available surface, including the
expensive fashion statements of several speechless
kids,

Who believe Ozzy when he calls me a clumsy waste of life,
all eyes turning in my direction as if I'm the one to
blame, and I know I'm beaten because as much as
I want to expel my fury right in his face, as much as
I want to play whack-a-mole on his hairless head, I
can't, and wouldn't they all laugh from here to the
edge of their miserable universe if they knew that the
boy most likely to fry was incapable of lifting a finger
to hurt anyone, even if the hurt was earned.

With nothing left but humiliation and red sauce, I just want
to escape, until Tennyson arrives out of nowhere,
barging his way between us, casting himself as an
unlikely avenger, and says,

"Got a problem, Ozzy?"

While the lazy-eyed lunch lady, out of touch with anything

on the far side of the warming trays, hands a plate of
ravioli to Ozzy, which Tennyson grabs from him and
gives to me, asking Ozzy if he plans to do anything
about it because, if he does, he should fill out his
complaint form in triplicate and shove them in all
three of his bodily orifices,

Which Ozzy has no comeback line for because he's still
trying to figure out which three orifices Tennyson
might be referring to, if he even knows what an
orifice is, and even though I don't want Tennyson
fighting my battles for me, I can't help but crack
a smile, because now I finally understand what it
means to have a friend, and maybe it's worth the
pain I'll endure because of it.

28) ANABOLIC

Chest press, shoulder press, lats press, squats;
Tennyson is all business in the gym,
>   *"Free weights are the way to go. Machines are for girls."*
Half an hour in, I'm feeling muscles I never knew I had.

Biceps, triceps, deltoids, pecs;
I am Tennyson's new project,
>   *"You need muscle mass to take on guys like Ozzy."*
Brontë might appreciate some muscle mass, too.

Crunches, curls, extensions, thrusts;
Tennyson is the trainer from hell,
>   *"You want something easier? Go pick flowers."*
He tells me it'll hurt even more tomorrow.

Low weight/high reps, high weight/low reps;
I'll learn to love the burn if I don't puke first,
    "You think this is hard? Wait till next time."
Tennyson says he'll make a bruiser out of me yet, and laughs.

Elevate heart rate, hydrate, repeat;
Better living through anabolic exercise,
    "Great workout," he says. "And I'm not even sore."
Right. Because I'm sore for both of us.

29) SURREPTITIOUS

Lacrosse,
Soccer's angry cousin,
Football's neglected stepchild.
No cheerleaders, band, or stands,
Games are played on the practice field
If you want a chair you bring your own,
Brontë waves,
She's saved me a spot,
It's Raptors versus Bulls,
Dinosaur against beast of burden,
I've never seen the game played before.
We turn to the match, which has already begun.
Tennyson
Is a starting attackman.

He's very good, but not great,
He's a fast runner, but not the fastest,
Still, he makes up for it in bullheaded aggression.
"He's always bucking for MVP," Brontë says,
    "but never gets it."
A pass,
He catches it
And moves downfield,
Cradling the ball in the net of his stick,
He shoots for the goal and misses by inches.
Then the Bulls power through the Raptor's defenses;
Goal.
Disappointment.
I feel Tennyson's frustration,
And I know that Brontë is right:
He'll be a team captain, but never the star,
Unless he has something to make him invincible.
I'm breathless
As I watch the game,
Then I suddenly realize why;
Tennyson *does* have a secret weapon
That can make him the star of the game.
I wonder what he'll do when he figures it out!
Stealing
The thunder

Of a stick check
To his right shoulder.
I bear the pain in silence
For fear that Brontë might see,
Scraped knee
Hidden by my jeans,
I could leave but choose to stay,
To surreptitiously sustain the blows,
Because if I am now Tennyson's project,
It's my right to make him my project as well.
Final whistle,
A Raptor victory!
Tennyson scored three goals,
And barely broke a sweat while doing it.
I kiss Brontë in the excitement of the moment.
Can she tell that I'm drenched beneath my Windbreaker?
And what if
When I get home,
Uncle Hoyt sees me,
Notices all the fresh bruises,
And knows that I've taken things,
From far beyond the bounds of our family?
I shudder
At the thought of him
Knowing about my secret life.

I could tell myself it would be all right,
That he could do no worse than he's already done,
But there's a pit in my uncle's soul,
and I've never seen the bottom.
I hope I never do.

30) STUFF

Brewster said I should always be the rag doll, but I never liked that much. I told him I'd rather be Plastic Boy instead, cuz that's a good name for a superhero.

"You're no superhero," Brew told me, "and don't go thinking that you are. Think *rag doll*, not superhero."

He says that cuza the time I jumped off the roof and broke his arm. Maybe he's right, though, on accounta I can't be Plastic Boy since I don't stretch. Still, I wish I could have myself a cooler secret identity for the times when Uncle Hoyt goes foul.

I wanted to tell Brontë-saurus about all that stuff, but Brew said, "A secret identity's gotta stay secret."

"Even from her?" I asked.

"*Especially* from her," he said—although I can't see why cuz they had been talking so much, it's like they're inside each other's brains.

Brontë-saurus swims good. I know this because of the time I taught her to do a cannonball, and then I beat her in a race across the pool. It was a great day, but it got a little scary because she saw all that stuff on Brew's body—the stuff we're not allowed to talk about, like my secret identity. She wanted to know how he got all the bruises—she thought it was Uncle Hoyt hitting him and stuff.

"Cody, does Uncle Hoyt beat me?" Brew asked me while looking in my eyes. "Tell the truth."

And so I did just like he wanted. I told the truth.

"No," I told Brontë-saurus, "Uncle Hoyt's afraid of Brewster," which is God's honest truth. Uncle Hoyt never hits Brew . . . but that's only a half of what the truth is, and a half-truth is worse than a lie cuz it's harder to figure out.

I could tell she knew something, but she didn't know what she knew. I could also tell that Brew wanted her all lost and confused about it, which meant they weren't inside each other's brains as much as I thought, which made me feel good.

That day at the pool was fine and sunny and cold, just like the day I'd jumped off the roof. That was back in first grade before I had any sense. See, I was tryin' to work my way up to it bit by bit. First I jumped from a chair, then I jumped from the porch, then I practiced jumping from the kitchen window over and over till I could do it and land on my feet easy.

The next step was the roof. That's what you call logic.

So I got the ladder out of the shed and climbed up there,

and I guess when I was climbin' that's when Brew got home from Saturday school—which he goes to a lot since he's always getting tardies because of the times Uncle Hoyt gets odd and won't let him leave the house in the morning.

The thing is, that day I took the ladder and climbed up on the roof, I didn't even know Brew was home. Wasn't like I did it on purpose. Wasn't like I knew we'd get hurt.

So there I was up on the roof doin' a countdown like they do for the space shuttle, and I was thinkin' that it was funny, cuz the space shuttle goes up and I'd be going down.

I had to do the countdown three times since I wasn't ready to jump the first two times, and once you scrub the mission you gotta start the countdown all over again. Finally, at the end of the third countdown, I jumped.

It felt like a thousand times higher than the kitchen window, and even though I landed on my feet, they slid out from under me because the ground was muddy. I put out my arms to catch myself and felt my right arm hit a big rock that was stickin' out of the ground, and I felt the bone snap—I think I even heard it, too.

I knew it was bad right away, and I was getting ready to feel the hurt that I knew would be coming, but it didn't come. Instead when I lifted my arm from the ground, the snap undid itself; and I heard Brewster screamin' bloodymurder in his bedroom, which woke Uncle Hoyt out of a deep sleep, and that's never a good thing.

"Cody!" my brother screams. "What did you do? What did you do?" And he comes out holding his arm, and I stand there and I explain how I had logically worked my way up to jumpin' off the roof, and I see how his arm's hangin' all wrong, and I know that I've done something bad.

Uncle Hoyt comes out, sees the arm, and now it's his turn to scream bloodymurder, cuz the last thing he wants is to drive Brewster to the hospital, but he does, because in the end Uncle Hoyt always does the stuff he's got to do even if he screams about havin' to do it.

Brew got a cast that went clear up to his elbow. Then he made me a cast, too, out of plaster and newspaper strips. He told me I was gonna wear it just like him because it would be the only way that I would ever learn. Only that didn't work out cuz my teacher found out that I was wearing a cast but didn't actually have a broken arm, and she called home and we all got called into the school, and Brew had to explain himself.

He said I jumped off the roof and landed on him, which was a lie but only a half-lie, which is just as hard to figure out as a half-truth. But my principal said that making me wear a cast without havin' no broken arm was child abuse. Since it was coming from another kid, though, they said that Brewster was just misguided. He said he was sorry, and he cut the cast off, and I swore up and down that I'd never jump off the roof again.

If Brew hadn't been there when I jumped, I would have owned that broken arm, all right—or at least I would have owned it until Brew got home and it became his. Either way it would have eventually been his broken arm, unless I runned away and stayed away months and months until my broken arm healed itself.

It's not like I don't know what it feels like to be hurt, though. I do get hurt when Brew's not around. A little bit, anyway. But Uncle Hoyt's good about making sure Brew stays home when we're not at school, so he's almost always around.

"Ain't safe for you out there," Uncle Hoyt's always saying to Brew. "So you do what you have to at school and get right home."

I got some friends from school, but Brew don't. "The kind of friends you get at school won't do you no good," Uncle Hoyt tells him. He don't know about Brontë-saurus.

Anyway, when Brew got his cast off, he put it on a shelf in our room as a reminder not to do dumb things. Most kids get their friends to write their names and stuff on their casts, but Brew said he didn't care enough about anybody to have their names on it.

Brewster's been hurtin' for me for as long as I can remember. There are times when he seems happy about it, but other times he's quiet and don't show no emotion at all. I keep being afraid he's gonna get angry the way Uncle Hoyt does, but Brewster never gets that angry—or if he does, he holds it all in until it goes away.

And it's true that Uncle Hoyt's afraid of him. He thinks Brewster must be an angel or the devil. Either way Brewster scares the heck out of Uncle Hoyt, and now that Brewster's bigger than him, I guess Uncle Hoyt's scared that one day Brewster will just haul off and knock him silly. Brewster's never done that though. Never hit a soul. Won't even kill a spider. I get spiders in my room all the time, and Brewster won't kill 'em.

"I care about nature," he says, and I guess because he cares about it he can't kill it, because if he cares about a spider and steps on it, he'd be killing a little bit of himself, too. He'd feel that spider dying under his feet. Maybe not as much as he feels the things that happen to the *people* he cares about, but still it's enough to make him catch all those spiders in glasses and shoo them outside.

I kill spiders though. Spiders and roaches and mosquitoes— it don't bother me at all cuz I care about nature, but only when it's outside.

Brew says he can't do violent stuff to crawly things or people, cuz his hand won't hit and his foot won't stomp, even when he wants them to. I think maybe he mighta been born that way. Or maybe he's just busted.

Once Brewster started spendin' all that time with Brontë-saurus (Brontë for short), it scared me a little. First, because if Uncle Hoyt found out he'd be mad, and second because

Brew doesn't get home from school right away. "I've got mandatory math tutoring," he told Uncle Hoyt, who believed it, and so Brew stays out with Brontë, and won't get home till maybe five or six—but I want Brewster home when I'm home because, see, Uncle Hoyt, he goes foul quite a lot these days. So far he's only gone foul when Brewster's been home, though. But what if something bad happens at work and Uncle Hoyt brings all that madness home with him, and can't sleep it off? Or what if he gets a letter from Aunt Debby's lawyer and he goes drinking so as to get himself nice and mean. That's why he drinks—he wants to get super-mean instead of just regular-mean, and he needs the alcohol to get there. It's like his mean-fuel. And then what am I gonna do if he starts to go foul and Brewster ain't here?

I told Brew about it on the way to school one day, how I was scared and all.

"Tell you what," Brewster said, "why don't you go to the library, and I'll come by and pick you up on my way home." So I started doing that, and it works real good. Sometimes he'll even pick me up from the library early, and we'll all go to the park, and Brontë will push me really high on the swing—higher than Brew does, because he's all worried I'll fly off and break his ribs or something.

There was this one day Brewster, Brontë, and me were at the park and she was pushing me on the swing, and she says to me, "I know about your brother."

I swing away, and when I swing back, I ask her, "Which part do you know?"

She seemed surprised by that. "There's more than one part?"

I knew I had to pick my words real careful here. "Well," I said, "do you mean the part about how he remembers everything, or the part about how he gets hurt for you?"

"Oh," she said, "both, I guess."

It didn't surprise me that Brontë knew. It was easy to keep secret from people Brew didn't like—but once he started liking you, you couldn't help but know. "Did he take something away for you?" I asked.

She nodded. "I hurt my ankle, and a gash on my hand."

"That was you? I wondered where he got those from—but Brew don't like me to ask, on accounta I might tell Uncle Hoyt by accident."

She got a little stiff at the mention of Uncle Hoyt. "Does your uncle know what Brew can do?"

"Yeah, he knows," I told her. "He's glad for it, I think," then I changed the subject, because Uncle Hoyt don't like to be talked about when he's not there. "Did Brew take other stuff from you?"

She seemed funny about answering that. "Not that I know of," she said, and I had to remind her to push me harder on the swing cuz her head was thinking about it.

"Sometimes," I told her, "he takes stuff away and you don't

even know. You never felt it so you don't know what you missed. But that only happens if he really cares about you. With me it's all automatic—I don't feel nothin'. Not even the time I fell into a beehive." Then I put down my landing gear in the sand and stopped swinging, getting all quiet, cuz a little kid and his mother just took over the swing next to ours and I didn't want them to hear. "We're not supposed to tell people about it," I told Brontë, "because people wouldn't understand. They'd take Brew away and stick tubes in him, and turn him into a weapon against terrorists and stuff."

She laughed at that, but I was serious.

"No one's taking him away," she said.

"But they might," I told her. "If they knew, they might. You didn't tell anyone did you?"

"No . . . but my brother knows," she said. "I promise neither of us will tell."

When Brew and I got home from the park, it was almost dark. By now Uncle Hoyt would be awake and getting ready for work. He'd be making us dinner, and breakfast for himself. He can cook a buncha things fast and good. Meat loaf, spaghetti—sometimes he even makes his own sauce. Although lots of times we get breakfast for dinner instead, because making two meals at once is just too much work for someone who just woke up.

When we went in, the house was mostly dark, and nothing was going on in the kitchen.

"Uncle Hoyt?" Brew called.

"Right here." We turned toward his voice, but it took a second until we saw him. He was sitting in a chair in the dark living room. "About time you two got home."

Another second and I could see him a little bit better. His knee was bouncing up and down like it does sometimes. He says it's coffee and stress that makes his knee bounce, but secretly I think it's us. Both Brew and I stood still, wondering if Uncle Hoyt sitting in a dark room was the start of something.

"Should I defrost some chicken for dinner?" Brew asked.

"You do that."

Brew turned on the kitchen light, and I got a look at Uncle Hoyt's eyes before he knew I was looking. He hadn't gone foul. Not today. He just looked worried. He'd just gone odd. Relieved, I got a drink from the sink while Brew took out frozen chicken pieces. Uncle Hoyt came to the doorway.

"I got an A on my spelling test," I told him.

"Good for you, Cody." But I could tell he wasn't really listening, so I put the test up on the fridge for him to see when he felt like noticing.

He watched Brew as my brother plugged up the sink and turned on the hot water. "I'm wondering if maybe you don't need all this tutoring," he said.

I could see Brew tense up just a little bit, and I sat at the kitchen table to get out of the line of fire.

"Can't do it by myself; math isn't my subject."

"I'll help you," Uncle Hoyt said.

"You know algebra?"

Uncle Hoyt's all insulted. "I'm not an idiot! I still remember it. And what I don't remember I can study up on."

I started wondering why Uncle Hoyt would do that when Brew can get free help at school. And then I remembered that Brew wasn't actually at math tutoring at all; he was with Brontë.

"And why would you need tutoring anyway?" Uncle Hoyt said. "You can near about memorize that math book just by lookin' at it."

"Words, not numbers," Brew said. "Numbers are different." Then he dropped the frozen chicken parts in the hot water to defrost. He didn't say anything else for a while. Sometimes it's best with Uncle Hoyt not to say much until you know exactly what he's thinking, and why.

"They shouldn't be making you spend so much time at school," he finally said. "It's not right. You should be with your family."

"Do you want to homeschool us like Mom did?" Brew asked.

"I didn't say that either."

Now it was Brew's leg that got the coffee-stress shake instead of Uncle Hoyt's.

"I'm worried about you, Brewski. That's all. You're never

here anymore. How can we be a family if you're never here?"

Brew turned off the tap but didn't look at Uncle Hoyt. "Sounds like you need a pet," he said. "Something that'll be waiting for you when you get up, and waiting for you to get home."

I liked the idea a lot. "Could we get a dog?" I asked. "I'll take care of it better than I took care of Tri-tip. I promise."

Uncle Hoyt smiled, but it wasn't a yes-smile. "You and Brew once had a dog back when your mom was alive," he said. "You were too little to remember, Cody; but I'll bet Brew does, don't you? You remember what happened to that dog?"

Brew put all of his thoughts on the chicken parts in the sink and didn't answer. Then Uncle Hoyt laughed big. He was changed from the time we came in. At first he was all nervous and squirrelly, but now he was proud and strutting and funny, like I like him to be. He even looked taller.

"Feeling better, Uncle Hoyt?" I asked.

"Cody," he said, "a million bucks ain't got nothin' on me." Which must mean yes. "You leave that chicken in the sink, Brew," he said. "I'll fry it up for us. I'll even save you the biggest piece."

Brew went to our room, practically knocking me over on his way out, and Uncle Hoyt went onto the porch to have a smoke. I brought my backpack into our room and saw Brew sitting on his bed, leaning against the wall like he's holding it up.

"You okay, Brew?"

"He's never gonna let me go, Cody." He rubbed his arms like he was cold; he rubbed his shoulder like it hurt. "He's gonna keep me here, taking his bursitis, his ulcers, and every one of his aches and pains."

"He's just protecting you," I reminded him.

"From what? From the world? From Brontë?"

I didn't have the answer, but the thought of Brewster going anywhere scared me.

"Why would you want to leave anyway?"

"Forget it," he said. "Go watch TV."

But I didn't. Instead I went out to sit with Uncle Hoyt on the porch, because he's nice to be around when he's in a good mood.

"This is how it should be," he said. "Sunset on the porch, and dinner in the oven."

"It's not in the oven yet."

He laughed, then got quiet for a second, taking a long puff on his cigarette. "Your brother doesn't really go to math tutoring, does he?"

Now I had to think up my own half-truth.

"I'm at the library," I told him. "I don't know who he's with."

"Ah! So he's *with* somebody!"

"No!" I told him, trying to back out of what I said, but sometimes words are like quicksand. "I said I don't know—I don't even know her name!"

He smiled the same smile as when he was talkin' about the dog. Since I didn't know what that smile meant, I slid just a little bit away from him in case my lying was reason to hit me, which it probably was.

"So," said Uncle Hoyt, "Brewski's got a girlfriend."

This time I just kept quiet, since the quicksand was already over my head.

"Bound to happen sooner or later," he said. "Just as long as she doesn't know about him and what he can do. Your brother's not stupid enough to tell her that."

He took his cigarette out of his mouth and studied it for a second—then he slowly lowered the lit end toward his arm, just beneath his elbow. He pressed the cigarette to his own skin. I gasped. He grimaced and hurled the cigarette away, cursing. There was a red spot on his arm, but only for a couple of seconds and then was gone.

And inside Brew screamed bloodymurder.

Uncle Hoyt brushed away the ash from his arm, which showed no sign of what he'd done.

"You see that, Cody?" he said. "It's *us* that Brew cares about, and God bless him for it. That girl is nothing, nothing at all. Now be a good boy and go tend to your brother."

I went inside to get the Band-Aids, glad that Uncle Hoyt kept his temper and didn't go foul.

TENNYSON

31) FORMIDABLE

If he touches her, I swear I'm going to brain him with my lacrosse stick and send what little gray matter comes out of his ears to the Smithsonian exhibit on prehistoric man.

What is my mother *thinking*? What's she even doing sneaking around with this guy? He's short, funny looking, and has no business eating meals in a public place with my mother—much less in an outdoor café where a person's offspring might walk by and see her. From what I can see, the only thing he's got going for him is hair, but so does a baboon. You can't even see his face beneath that stupid beard—not that I'd want to. And why does he keep picking at that greasy facial hair anyway? What's he looking for, lice?

How am I supposed to focus on today's game with the image of them sharing a crème brûlée burned into my retinas like a cattle brand? I know she must have seen me. And I know she won't say anything about it when I get home tonight.

The only shred of hope is that the suitcases are still in the basement, and nobody's packing. Sure, Dad's moved into the guest room—but he did that last year when he was the one sharing desserts with a total stranger. "This will pass," I tell myself. I just wish I could believe it.

But I've got to put it out of my mind—I have a game to think about.

We're on a winning streak, and I intend to keep it that way.

When I get to the field, Katrina's there to cheer me on, along with Ozzy O'Dell and his stupid swim-shaved body and a half-dozen other classmates. What interest Ozzy has in lacrosse, I haven't got a clue. I really don't feel like talking to anyone right now, but Katrina comes up to me.

"So Mr. Martinez is all like '¿Dónde está su tarea?' and Ozzy'd memorized like ten different excuses for not having his homework—in perfect Spanish—so nobody else in the class knows what he's saying; but it makes Mr. Martinez laugh so hard, he's all like 'That's even better than homework'—and not only does Martinez give Ozzy a homework pass, he gives him *extra crédito*, which is extra credit in Spanish, and— Tennyson, are you even listening to me?"

"Yeah, yeah. Extra credit. Very funny."

In my current state of mind, the last thing I want to do is play lacrosse against the Gators, whose sportsmanship quotient is one step below the World Wrestling Federation. They send someone to the hospital every other game. But I've been hot for the past few games—strong and focused—playing better than I've ever played before. I can't let this whole thing with Mom take away my edge.

Brontë shows up, I think because she'd rather be here than at home these days. I'm about to tell her that I saw Mom with some short, hairy guy, but I decide to spare her the pain.

"Let me see your knuckles," she says.

I groan in frustration. "They're the same. Healed. So leave me alone—I don't go asking to look at your nonexistent cut, so don't insist on seeing my nonexistent scabs."

Brontë finds it amazing that I can just accept Brewster's ability without question.

"How could you not be freaked out by the impossible?"

"He does it," I tell her, "so obviously it's not impossible."

My answer just infuriates her. I love it when that happens.

The truth is, I don't have room in my skull to spend endless hours obsessing over what Brewster can do. I have enough to deal with, between school, lacrosse, and the fact that Dad sleeps on a foldout and Mom's having lunch with the Missing Link. What's worse is that Mom and Dad won't talk about what's going on. In my book that's far more surreal than anything Brew can do.

The game begins and I get right into it, living in the moment, putting everything else out of my mind. I'm an attackman—the front offensive line—and the Gators are a formidable foe. I've got to be quick and alert if I'm going to score against them.

The whistle blows, and we scrap for the ball. One of our midfielders gets it and passes to me. I tear down the field, cradling the ball in the pocket of my stick. I dodge the Gators' defenders and toss it to our right wing—who should pass it back to me, since I've got a clean shot; but instead he goes for it himself, and misses by a mile.

The Gators' keeper is on it in an instant and hurls the ball deep into our territory. It suddenly strikes me that even though Brontë is here, neither of my parents has made it to a game this year.

Suddenly the whistle blows. The Gators have scored. I was so distracted by my own thoughts, I didn't even see it, and I'm furious at myself. I have to stay focused!

"Don't worry," I call to my teammates. "It's just the first quarter. We'll get it back!"

I line up for the face-off, taking my anger and molding it until I'm a controlled ball of fury, using the lost goal to propel me toward victory.

With possession of the ball again, I barrel through an opening, toward the Gators' goal. I'm almost there when out of my blind spot one of their defenders races in to me. He's big, beefy, and checks me so hard I go flying. There's a pain in my gut and panic in my chest, like the air has been sucked from the planet. The wind's been knocked out of me, and I know

I'm going to be down for a good thirty seconds.

But that's not what happens. Instead the miserable feeling is gone in an instant. Maybe it's all the working out I'm doing, because my stomach muscles held out the worst of it. It's been that way for a few games now. Less exhaustion, quicker recovery on the field. I've hit my stride this year!

The ball's still in my stick, I'm back on my feet, I fire it, the goalie dives, but he's nowhere close.

Goal!

Cheers from the sidelines. Now I'm in the zone, and nothing else matters. This game is mine!

I'm still on fire in the second period.

We let one goal slide—but I score another, tying the game at 2–all. One of the Gators' midfielders elbows me hard, out of view of the refs. I feel a sudden sharp pang in the ribs. I grimace—but the pain is gone in just a few seconds. I've willed it away!

Halftime.

Used to be I'd feel the strain of all the exertion by now, but lately it's like I can run the field forever and never get tired. The coach, who usually pulls me out for the third quarter, sees I'm riding a wave again and keeps me in. *I'm* the formidable foe the Gators need to look out for now!

Third quarter.

The score is 4 to 2. I've scored three of our goals. The Gators are getting nervous, playing sloppy, fouling like mad. I intercept a pass from their goalie and power toward the goal—but it's not gonna happen. Not this time, because one of their defenders plants his foot right in front of me—an intentional trip—and I fly, my stick launching away from me. I hear the whistle blow even before I hit the ground. It'll cost them a penalty shot; but when I come down, I come down wrong. My head hits at a strange angle, my helmet connecting with a rock that's hidden in the turf. Not even the helmet is enough to protect me from the concussive shock of coming down right on my head.

I can feel my brain rattled, but I regain my senses quickly. Too quickly. How could I not have been hurt by that? I'm up, bouncing on the balls of my feet in seconds—even the refs are surprised.

And that's when I see him.

Brewster is here. He's on the sideline and he's doubled over, lying on his side in pain. Brontë fusses over him; and suddenly I know why my ribs had hurt for only an instant, and why the wind didn't get knocked out of me, and why my muscles feel none of the ache of three quarters of play. Because Brewster's feeling it for me. He's feeling it all—and not just today, but for every game he's been at. It's not my skills that are putting me at the top of my game. It's Brewster.

The ref starts play again—I even get a penalty shot and score—but I can't focus now. I just keep looking over to the sideline until Brew sits up again, recovering from my fall. He might have my concussion for all I know.

The coach takes me out for half of the fourth quarter, then puts me back in toward the end of the game; but I'm not the player I was ten minutes ago. Now I'm way too cautious, way too slow—because what if I get hurt again? What if I take a blow and Brew absorbs it again? I can't allow that. So for the last five minutes of play, I just go through the motions, half-heartedly crossing the field like my body is made of eggshells and will fracture with the slightest contact.

The final whistle blows. We win, 5 to 2. I'm the hero of the team, but it feels empty. It feels like I cheated. Like the game was rigged, and I'm the only one who knows. Everyone's giving me slaps on the back and high fives—and no one seems to notice how I shut myself down in the final minutes. They probably figure I just got tired from playing so hard.

The second I can break away from my teammates I tear off my helmet and storm toward Brewster. He's standing with Brontë, cheering like the rest of them—but I can see the evidence of this vicious game all over him; and maybe I should feel grateful, but all I feel is angry. Angry and robbed. I'd rather play hard and lose honestly than suffer such a despicable win. He stole more than my pain today.

"Tennyson, you were great," Brontë says. At first I think she must not get it—she must be clueless; but no, my sister is smart. And suddenly it dawns on me that she knows! Maybe from the first game, or maybe just from today. She knows, and yet she's okay with it. How could she be okay with it?

I storm toward Brewster, and I raise my hand—I almost punch him—but I can't swing at someone who already looks so beaten down. Instead I point an accusing finger and burn him a brutal scowl.

"Never come to one of my games again!" I snarl.

"You won, didn't you?"

"No, I didn't win—*you* did." And I storm away, leaving everyone around us gawking.

Katrina tries to intercept me. "Something wrong, Tennyson?"

But I'm not in the mood. "I gotta go back to the team." Then I run onto the field, trying to put as much distance as I can between me and Brewster Rawlins.

32) CONTRITION

"I'm sorry," I tell Brontë for the tenth time.

"Don't tell me; tell *him*."

"I will. On Monday."

"No! You go over to his house and tell him right now!"

"I don't want to go over there!" I shout at her. "I don't want to deal with his crazy, freaking uncle!"

I take a deep breath and pace the living room. Mom has not come home yet, and I can't help but wonder if she's still visiting the Planet of the Apes. Dad, who spends more and more time at the university lately, is AWOL as well. It's not that I want them here at the moment, but I don't want them out there, either.

"I will hound you day and night until you apologize to him!"

I really want to strangle my sister right now, but I restrain myself. *"Your temper is not your friend,"* my kindergarten teacher used to tell me. It annoys me that I still remember that, down to her squeaky little voice. It annoys me more that she was right.

"I need to sort things out, okay?" I say to Brontë, trying to sound as reasonable as I can. "If I go over there now, even if I say I'm sorry, I might end up fighting with him about it more."

"Why? What did he do that was so terrible?"

The fact that she can't see my side of it boggles the mind. "He *felt* stuff for me!" Even saying it makes me uneasy, like it's some sort of violation—and in some ways I guess it is. "I got hurt out there on the field, but all that hurt kept vanishing into him! It's not *normal*!"

Now she's smiling—even gloating. "It's about time you freaked out about it."

"Shut up!"

"He likes you, Tennyson. You may be the first real friend he's ever had."

"That still doesn't give him the right to reach inside me. Maybe you're okay with it, being that you're his girlfriend and all; but I'm not."

"It's not like he's doing it on purpose; he can't help it. It just happens."

"He should have warned me—or he should have left!"

"He didn't want to. It was his choice to stay."

"Well, he should have given *me* a choice!" I can hear my voice rising again as I think back to the game. It's great to get all the glory when you've earned it; but when you haven't, you feel like a fraud. Maybe other guys get their kicks by seizing attention they don't deserve, but not me. "All I'm saying is that you can't play a sport without the threat of injury! It's like they say, 'No pain, no gain'—without the pain, the gain means nothing!"

Brontë weighs my words and nods, finally admitting that maybe I have a point. "Fine. So explain that to him."

"I will when I can stop yelling!"

Then Brontë, bless her annoying little heart, says the exact thing to put out my fire. She heaves a colossal sigh and says, "Listen to us! We sound like Mom and Dad."

And since that's the last act in the world I want to mimic, my anger is snuffed so completely, all that remains is an intense desire to pout.

"Are we done here?" I ask.

"Yes. But don't stay mad at him," she says. "That will hurt him worse than any lacrosse game."

33) QUIETUS

Mom and Dad come home within fifteen minutes of each other, both the bearers of ethnic takeout. Mom has Chinese; Dad has Indian. It's a strange thing for your parents to be sort of separated but living under the same roof. Brontë and I still get the same fast food, but now there's always twice as much, because both of them feel obliged to feed us. It's fine when the food comes staggered; but at times like this, when it comes simultaneously, it's very awkward. Whose food do we eat? And does it imply we're taking sides? Can we eat equal portions of both without feeling like puking? When an eggroll becomes a crisis, there's definitely something wrong.

That night I lie on my bed bloated beyond belief, having eaten enough to feed an entire subcontinent. My brain is bloated, too, and I try to wrap my mind around the events of the day.

I'm not usually one to spend endless hours dissecting my own emotions. Brontë does enough of that for both of us. When it comes to such open-heart reflection, I'm a firm believer in the observer effect, which states that anything you try to observe is automatically changed by the mere fact that you're looking at it. The way I see it, if you try to study your emotions on a microscopic level, the best you can do is understand how it feels to hold the magnifying glass.

As I lie there listening to India and China waging war in my intestines, I keep trying to analyze the feelings I had at the end of today's lacrosse game. Perhaps it's just the observer effect and my perceptions are all changing as I examine them, but it seems to me there was something inexplicable running under the anger I felt toward Brewster. Kind of like the undertow tugging at your feet even as the wave slams into you.

What I felt was this: an unexpected quietus of everything bad I was feeling. An extinguishing of all my anger and frustration. The numbing came just as I told off Brewster. Once I vented at him, I couldn't hold on to my rage. By the time I had stormed back to the team, I was feeling okay about everything. But feeling "okay" was absolutely wrong — it felt like another level of fraud on my part.

I saw him hurrying away then. Hurrying away in fury. Was he angry at me for being angry at him? Maybe. Or maybe it was more than that.

That's the real reason why I don't want to face Brewster quite yet. Because I'm not sure whether it's just me being weird . . . or if that undertow is the first hint of a much more powerful riptide.

34) TRAJECTORY

Once in a while Dad and I go out to shoot some hoops. He does this because basketball is the only sport where he still has a fighting chance against me since he still has a height advantage. Early on Sunday morning I go over to Brew's place and invite him to join us. It's my way of apologizing, because the actual words *I'm sorry* don't come easy to me—unless, of course, I'm saying it to Brontë. It seems I'm always apologizing to her.

We're on his porch, because Uncle Hoyt is sleeping after a hard night flattening asphalt. Cody's out in their ugly acre trying to fly a cheap cellophane kite; but the weeds are too tall, and he can't get up enough momentum when he runs.

"Consider it the next phase of our workouts," I tell Brew. "Basketball builds agility—you can't get that with free-weights."

"Aren't you worried you'll skin your elbows and make me bleed?"

To which I respond, "Are you calling me a klutz?" It then occurs to me for the first time why he seemed so exhausted after our weight-lifting sessions and why I didn't. I start to feel ticked off that he never said anything; but I let it go, because anger is not our friend.

"Thanks for the invitation," Brewster says, "but I can't. My uncle likes weekends to be family time." Which is ridiculous, considering the man has a night job and sleeps all day. "It's easier for everyone if I just stay home."

"Easier doesn't make it right," I point out. And then I hear a voice from behind me.

"Tell Uncle Hoyt you won't like him no more."

I turn to see Cody standing there holding that sorry little kite. It's a typical thing for a little kid to say; but Brew seems to be struck by the words, like they contain divine wisdom. I have no idea why a man like Uncle Hoyt would care what Brew thought of him.

Brew reaches to a Band-Aid on his forearm. I wonder what kind of wound it conceals. He rubs the wound, mulling over what Cody said. Then he turns to me. "Which park will you be at?"

I don't know exactly what Brew says to Uncle Hoyt, but the result is that both Brewster and Cody show up at the park. My dad and I are feeling pretty down, although we try not to show it. Mom wasn't home when we left; I suspect she's probably off with her boyfriend, the Muppet. I have no idea whether she's in the process of breaking it off, making it stick, or just escaping from everything. I don't think Dad knows either. A cloud of gloom follows us to the court, but when Brew arrives, it seems to dissipate. Maybe because there's someone else to focus on.

Cody immediately escapes from the court, having no use whatsoever for basketball. He's much more engaged by a malfunctioning sprinkler head in the grass.

It's immediately clear to Dad and me that Brew's experience in basketball is limited to the wonderful world of phys ed. He can dribble standing still, and he has just the right trajectory on his foul shots to sink some of them; but he lacks any real-world game.

"Didn't you ever shoot around with your uncle?" Dad asks, completely oblivious to the Uncle Hoyt situation.

"My uncle is more of a baseball kind of guy."

And that's all my dad needs to hear. Brew is hoop impoverished. Suddenly my dad's in his element; and for the first time in years, the teacher in him has a blank athletic slate—a new subject to whom he can impart all the family basketball moves.

"You know, I played in college," Dad brags, doing some Globetrotter stuff that was only impressive the first hundred times—but Brew's eating it up. Even Cody looks up from his irrigation project as Dad deftly handles the ball. I suppress the urge to roll my eyes, hoping that someday my own children will return the favor.

"Stick with me," Dad says, "and you'll own the court in no time."

It feels good to see my father in this altered state—actually enjoying himself, with no thoughts of Mom and the nest of termites that's eating away at the foundation of our family. In fact, none of that seems to bother me either. It all feels far, far away.

Brew—with that photographic memory of his—is a quick study. By the time we're done for the day, he's got himself a respectable layup and can guard without fouling.

"Thank you, Mr. Sternberger." His gratitude is genuine.

"Not a problem, Brewster."

"Call me Brew."

It feels good to be out here and away from all the frustrations of life. In fact, the entire day feels abnormally good in a way I can't quite describe. It's that quirky kind of weekend feeling they write ridiculous sunny-day songs about. You know the ones—I'm sure they're on your iPod even though you'd never admit it. As for my father, he's more up than I've seen him in weeks.

"An hour on the court puts things into perspective," Dad

says as he hands the ball to Brew for a final shot. "I have a feeling things are just going to get better."

It turns out he's right. And at the same time very, very wrong.

CODY

35) STUFF

Uncle Hoyt had a bad day the next week. He hadn't had a real bad day for a while. Sure, he was always grumpy, but grumpy wasn't foul. There were times when he was actually nice—like the night Tri-tip had died and he read me *Goodnight Moon* and a bunch of other little-kid books, and actually even kissed me good night.

"Don't you worry about Tri-tip," he'd told me, "he's gone to a better place."

Well, since I heard a chain saw going for two whole hours, I knew that the "better place" didn't take a dead bull whole; but I guess he musta meant cow heaven.

That was a side of our uncle we didn't see all that often, but it was good to see it when we did. Those are the times I always try to hold on to when he goes foul.

Like he did when his steamroller hit a car.

I wasn't there when it happened, since he's not allowed to

ever take me to work, even on Take Your Kid to Work Day, cuz the work is dangerous and he usually does it at night. I found out the next day, when I got home from school.

It was Thursday, and Brew was out with Brontë at the mall. I wanted to go, but Brew said I wasn't invited this time. He wasn't even makin' up stories for Uncle Hoyt anymore—not since last Sunday when he'd played basketball with Tennyson and his father. Things changed a little bit on that day. See, Uncle Hoyt wasn't gonna let us go anywhere that morning, but Brew said he was gonna go out anyway.

"Where are you going? Who you gonna be with?" Uncle Hoyt had asked, but all Brew said was "None of your business, and none of your business."

I expected Uncle Hoyt to start yelling, but he just said, "Careful there, Brew." I couldn't tell whether he meant to be careful out there, or be careful of him.

Then Brew showed him the cigarette burn and said, "One of these days you're gonna test me, and there'll be no one getting hurt but you."

"Is that a threat, boy?"

"No, just the truth. I don't know how I could go on caring about someone who won't even let me have my own life."

Even though it was my idea for Brew to tell Uncle Hoyt he wouldn't like him no more, I never thought it would be such a big deal. Before it could get any worse, I shouted out, "Basketball! Brew and me are just going to the park for some basketball."

Uncle Hoyt nodded but kept his eyes stuck on Brew. "Fine, then," he said, but his voice didn't say it was fine at all. "You want what's out there, you go grab it, boy. Just don't say I didn't warn you."

Ever since then things haven't been right between them. They don't fight, but they don't talk much either; and when they're in the same room, I feel like I don't want to be there.

So anyway, it's Thursday night, and it's getting dark, and I come inside from tryin' to fly that stupid kite again; but now it's got so many holes, the wind couldn't pick it up even if it wanted to cuz it would just blow through the holes. Once I'm inside, I can hear Uncle Hoyt all worked up on the phone. He's pacing the kitchen, shouting about an accident he had the night before, explaining how it wasn't his fault. A car veered over the cones and hit his steamroller, not the other way around. But I guess that doesn't matter—someone has to get blamed. From what I can hear, a person is in the hospital. Stable condition, which I guess is better than dead.

I did believe Uncle Hoyt when he said he didn't do nothing wrong, because if there's one thing he's proud of, it's the way he drives that steamroller. He drives it like there's no one else in the world can do it as good as him.

So I'm standing in the living room, listening to him on the phone; but he's already been drinking, and he's slurring his words. I don't think that helps things. From what Uncle Hoyt yells into the phone, I know that his boss has taken him off the roller and has given him the lowest job in road construction.

"Pushing tar?" he says. "I've been at this for years, and you're making me push tar?" I hear some yelling on the other end of the phone, and then Uncle Hoyt says, "Fine, then I won't come in at all."

When Uncle Hoyt hangs up, he doesn't just hang up; he hurls the phone at the refrigerator and it shatters into a gazillion pieces. That's when he notices me standing there, watching him.

"What are you looking at?" he says. "Go do your homework."

"I got none," I tell him.

"Then just get out of my sight."

"You gonna get fired, Uncle Hoyt?"

"Get outta here!"

I don't need another invitation. I go to my room while Uncle Hoyt keeps on drinking. All the while I keep looking out of my window at the empty field and the fence and the houses beyond that, looking for Brew, hoping he'll get home soon. I know he's still out with Brontë. There's no telling when he'll get back. And I get to thinking that part of Uncle Hoyt's bad mood is my fault, because I told Brew to say he wouldn't like him no more. If I hadn't done that, Brew would be home now instead of off with Brontë; and if he was home, maybe Uncle Hoyt might not be so mad.

Right around sunset—the time Uncle Hoyt would usually

be leaving for work—he goes out onto the porch instead. I can hear the squeak of the folding chair as he sits down and starts talking. He's talking to nobody, having conversations with himself—all the things he wishes he could say to his boss and everyone else but doesn't have the guts to actually say. He's still chewing out his boss to the crickets when I get up to go to the bathroom.

I should have known what would happen next, and if I had been thinking ahead, I could have stopped it. See, he's outside and I'm inside, and just last week our screen door handle busted. You can push it open from the inside, but once you're outside you can scratch and paw at that door all you want; it's near impossible to open—and totally impossible if you're drunk.

"Cody!" I hear him call, but I'm still in the bathroom, taking care of business.

"Cody," he calls again, "open the stupid door!"

And I'm hurrying as fast as I can to get off the pot, but there's only so fast you can do such a thing. By the time I'm out of the bathroom, he's screaming bloodymurder; and when I get out into the living room, I can see him through that screen.

His eyes.

I know those eyes.

Uncle Hoyt's gone foul, and Brew is nowhere to be seen, and I don't know what I'm gonna do, so I just stand there staring at him, afraid to open that door, knowing it's only going to make it worse; but still I just stand there anyway, watching those eyes get fouler and fouler as he screams, "Open this goddamn door!" Finally he punches his fist through the screen and reaches inside, pulling the door open.

Now there's nothing between him and me.

I start backing up—I think that maybe I can run out the back door—but Uncle Hoyt's fast for a drunken man. Before I can make a move, he's there. He grabs at me—missing mostly, but catching enough of my shirt to get me off balance. I fall, hitting the edge of the TV, and I know that Brew isn't anywhere close because it hurts!

"You think that was funny, huh?" he growls. "Letting me stand out there? Had yourself a laugh, did ya?"

He gets a good grip on me this time, and I think, *Rag doll, rag doll, be the rag doll*, just like Brew always tells me; but I can't do it because Brew isn't here. Uncle Hoyt tosses me, though, like I really am a rag doll. I think maybe he's aiming for the sofa; but I miss and hit the table beside it, knocking over a lamp. The bulb blows out, and I wish I woulda been more careful, because Uncle Hoyt's gonna blame me for that just like his boss blames him for that car hittin' his steamroller.

"You're useless," he shouts. "You're useless!" because when he's drunk, Uncle Hoyt says lots of things twice. "You and your brother, both! He thinks he can go out there and do whatever he wants? If it wasn't for the two a you, I'd have a life! You both owe me! You owe me everything!" And now I know this is my fault, because it's Brew he's mad at even more than me, but I'm the one who's here and Brew's not, and it's all because of me.

He moves closer. I can see his right hand clenching into a fist, and I know he's gonna use it, so I reach for something—anything—and I find a glass ashtray on the table next to me, all square and heavy, and I throw it at Uncle Hoyt. I don't know what an ashtray is going to do to stop him; all I know is I gotta do something.

It hits him on the forehead with a *bonk* that I can hear, and in a second there's blood on his forehead. The way he looks at me now makes me think that maybe I just ended my own life.

"Did you just throw that at me?" he says, all amazed. "Did you just throw that at me?"

And my own mind is such a knot, I shake my head and say, "No, sir," like denying it might calm him down; but I know it won't do no good, because Uncle Hoyt had a bad day, and now my day's gonna be even worse than his.

I scramble away toward that screen door. I can push it open from the inside easy, but he grabs my foot and pulls me back before I get there.

"You are going to be sorry you did that, boy," he says. "I am going to teach you to respect me. You hear me? You hear me?"

He reaches to pull his belt out of his pants, but his belt

isn't there—and he knows if he goes to find it, I'll get free, so he doesn't let go. He picks me up, carrying me like a football. There's nothing I can do but kick and squirm.

"I'm gonna teach you a lesson. Both of you. Two birds with one stone. He don't want to be here; he'll pay the consequences!"

In a second we're outside, and I can see the screen door banging closed behind us, getting farther away.

"You'll learn to respect me!"

The way he's holding me I can see where we been but not where we're going. But I know without having to see. It's the same place he always takes me when he goes foul. There's a shed way back at the edge of our property. It's the place farthest away from any other homes, so you can't hear much of what goes on in there. Not that our neighbors would care. Not that our neighbors even know us.

There's no way out of this, and I'm scared. More scared than I've ever been in my life. Not even when they told me about Mom dying and all I wasn't this scared because I didn't understand that then—I was too little. But this I understand. And although Uncle Hoyt has needed to teach me lessons before, he's never been this foul—and it never happens without Brew.

Tonight it's going to be bad.

Uncle Hoyt opens the door to the shed with his free hand and closes it behind him. Then he pulls a string dangling from up above and a light comes on. The first things I see are the tools on the wall: hammers, screwdrivers, shovels. A wild part of me thinks that Uncle Hoyt might use them; but there's crazy and there's *crazy*, and Uncle Hoyt isn't *crazy*. He ain't no murderer. Or if he is, he's an accidental one, because although I know he means to teach me proper respect, tonight he might teach it too well.

"Please, Uncle Hoyt!" I beg. "Wait till morning—lessons are best in the morning, right?"

"You've got it coming," he says, staggering. "You got it coming *now!*"

I try to hide underneath the workbench. It's full of webs and bugs down there, but I don't care about those, not now. I squeeze all the way into the corner, but he reaches right in and grabs my leg, and drags me out. I feel the concrete floor scraping my elbows; and as he pulls at me, I bite his arm with all the force that I can, figuring it might sober him up. He curses and swings me a backhanded slap across my face. It's the first time he's actually hit me tonight; but it won't be the last, because I know the first one makes all the rest easier. My face stings, and I'm crying now, which is bad because my eyes are all clouded and I can't see straight enough to move out of the way of his swinging hands. I think if I'm fast enough and he's drunk enough I can dodge the worst of it, like in dodgeball. I never get hit in dodgeball, but I can't dodge nothin' with blurry eyes.

"I never wanted you," Uncle Hoyt slurs. "Neither of you. Neither of you."

Hearing it woulda hurt awful if he hadn't already said that a hundred times—and if I didn't know that only a part of him means it anyway.

"It shouldn't never have been this way," he says as he grabs me again. "But if it's got to be, then you've got to learn to treat me the way you woulda treated your own father."

I push out of his grip again and bounce against the wall. Tools fall around me, clattering to the ground. My back should hurt from hitting the wall so hard, but it doesn't. Not just that, but the stinging on my face from the slap is fading much faster than it should.

And that's when I know.

That's when I know he's there.

Brew's come home to save me! I look up to the little window, and I can see him there outside. Just a hint of his face in the darkness, looking in on us.

He doesn't kick down the door or nothin'. He doesn't come in to stop Uncle Hoyt. He never does. He says he can't, but what he can't do don't matter. Just what he *can* do. And he's doing it now.

But Uncle Hoyt doesn't know yet.

"Get up!" Uncle Hoyt says to me.

But I don't. Instead I do what I have to do. I become the rag doll, falling limp on the floor, pretending I got no bones. Pretending I got no flesh—just stuffing sewed up in cloth.

A second more and Uncle Hoyt knows Brew is there,

because that little cut on his forehead where the ashtray hit him slowly zips itself closed. It don't happen as fast as it does for me, because Brew don't care about Uncle Hoyt as much as he cares about me. But he cares about him enough, because that wound is gone; and Uncle Hoyt knows it, because now his anger moves away from me to Brew, and Uncle Hoyt sees him in the window.

"Finally came back, did ya!" Uncle Hoyt growls like a bear if a bear could speak. "Well, you're too late! Let the boy take his own due."

But Brew stands there, stone-faced, and won't say a word.

"Just as well. This is for both of you then."

That's when Uncle Hoyt starts to use his fists, taking everything out on me, but it's nothing to me cuz I'm the rag doll.

I hear grunts from outside. Not screams, because Brew, he's good at holdin' it all in, keepin' it all to himself. I know how much it must hurt, and it just makes Uncle Hoyt angrier that I'm not getting his lesson. He screams and curses, wishing I was, but knowing I'm not.

I close my eyes and stay limp, bouncing and flopping around the shed, lettin' him kick, and hit, and pull, and tug. I even start smiling, like it's all just a whole lot of rocking in a crib. *You can't hurt me, Uncle Hoyt, no matter how foul you get, because I've got Brew to protect me. And he'll never let you hurt me. Never never never.*

BREWSTER

36) RECEIVER

I stayed out till dark,
And my brother went home alone,
To face our worst nightmare.
Now I stand at the shed window
Until my legs give out.
My uncle is a weapon turned on my brother.
Now turned on me.

> *"Let the boy take his own due."*

But I won't allow it, and he knows it.
Is it me my uncle beats?
Is his foot so swift,
Are his hands so furious
Because he knows it's coming to me?
For being disloyal?
For wanting more than this?
Or is he furious at the futility,

Furious at knowing
He will never teach us to respect him?
The muddy ground,
All fours,
I roll to my side,
Ear in mud,
Knee to chest,
I swallow my screams.
Forcing them into my stomach.
Digest the pain.
Dissolve it,
Then sweat it out,
Piss it out,
Wetness spreading in my jeans,
As foul as my uncle,
Who I should hate,
But can't.
Who I should stop,
But can't.
This wiring inside me is all wrong.
I'm built to receive.
I can't kill an ant,
I can't salt a snail,
I can't raise a hand to my uncle,
My wiring won't let me.
So I lie in the mud,

In my pain,
In my weakness,
And my fury at him
Is nothing compared to my fury at myself.

I am the crumbling aftermath of the earthquake.
The dust settling over the ruins.
Three minutes and it's over.
I rise, battered but not broken.
Never broken.
It will take more than my uncle to do that.
I reach for the rusted knob,
Opening to find Cody,
His hair a wild mess,
Eyes frightened and lost,
But not a mark upon him.
And Uncle Hoyt
Has crumbled, too.
Ruined and rocking,
A baying, keening ball of misery,
Kneeling in the center of the shed,
Gripping himself as if he's the one in pain.

> *"I'm sorry, I'm sorry, I'm sorry!"* he wails.
> *"I didn't mean it! I didn't mean any of it.*
> *I'm sorry, I'm sorry, I'm sorry!"*

Always the same.

He means it, too.
He means it in the moment.
But that doesn't change what he's done.
To Cody.
To me.
I take my brother and close the door on Uncle Hoyt,
Escaping from the epicenter
Because I can feel my uncle's pain,
Like worms in my flesh.
But if I can get far enough away,
Fast enough away,
His agony will be his, and his alone.

Our bedroom is my sanctuary.
I take off my shirt.
I lie facedown on my bed.
We begin the ritual.
Cody and I.
We both know it well.
A warm, wet cloth begins it.
He mops it across my back.
Gently tracing reconnaissance of the wounds.
             "Is there bleeding?"
          "No," Cody says. *"A little."*
He wipes my face,
Around my swelling eyes,

And in his eyes I see how bad it is.
A second cloth,
This one with alcohol.
Cold and stinging.
I swallow this pain, too.
The next cloth is dry.
Cody carefully blots,
He assesses,
He's strategic with Band-Aids,
Familiar with the shapes and sizes.

"You want a shirt?"

"Not yet."

He puts a towel across my back,
Maybe to keep me warm,
Maybe to hide the scars of battle.

"They should be mine."

"Don't say that. Don't ever say that."

He nods and begins to cry,
But it only lasts an instant,
Because before a single tear falls
His sorrow becomes mine,
A heaviness in my heart,
A salty sting in my eyes.

"I want to be sad," he says. *"Can't you let me feel sad?"*
But I can't do that.
I'm not wired that way.

I dream of the morning,
And how it will unfold.
Uncle Hoyt never remembers;
It's very convenient.
He'll grasp just enough to know he did something wrong,
But not enough to take responsibility for it.
Cody will avoid his eyes at breakfast,
Studying his Alphabits like they're a spelling test;
But I'll hold my uncle's gaze,
Making him look away,
Because this time was worse than all the others,
And he'll know,
And he'll have to remember,

> *"Let me see it,"* he'll say.

He'll reach for my shirt, but I'll pull away,
The wounds are my dignity; I will not share them.
And that's when he'll get scared.

> *"You won't tell no one, right?*
> *If you do they'll ask questions,*
> *You'll have to give answers,*
> *They'll take you away,*
> *Then you and your brother,*
> *They'll split you both up,*
> *That's what they do,*
> *Is that what you want?*
> *So you don't gotta tell,*

'Cause who would believe it,
This thing you can do?
And what happened last night
Won't happen again,
See, I've learned my lesson,
I'm making amends,
We're a family here,
It's nobody's business,
A family, Brew,
Let's keep it that way."

I'm ready to face him when morning comes,
Ready for all those things he'll say.
I rise with bold and righteous indignation,
The wounds on my body an accusation,
I'm ready!
But Uncle Hoyt cannot be roused,
His stupor extends into the day,
His snores shake the house,
And confronting a sleeping man
Is no confrontation at all,
So I get Cody breakfast
And gingerly slip my backpack
Over aching shoulders,
Then we head off to school,
Both of us knowing
That we won't tell a soul.

37) PHOSPHORESCENCE

The way I see it, the impossible happens all the time; but we're so good at taking it for granted, we forget it was once impossible.

I mean, look at airplanes—come on, how could they *not* be impossible? These gigantic metal things you'd need a massive hydraulic winch just to get off the ground? Please! They used to say, *"If man were meant to fly, he'd have wings"*; but it didn't stop poets from dreaming, did it? Then a few hundred years ago a man named Bernoulli came up with an elegant mathematical principle about pressure, air density, and velocity—and bingo! Poetry became poetry in motion, and now objects bigger than blue whales are filling the friendly skies, thank you very much.

I think small children are far more in tune with the wonder of it all, far better than the rest of us more "sensible" and "mature" folk. They look at every little thing, from fireflies to lightning, and stand in awe that such things exist. Sometimes we need to be reminded that that's how we *should* feel . . . but, on the other hand, if we felt that way all the time, we'd just marvel at the fireworks and never get anything done.

I will reluctantly admit that I am also a victim of species numbness. I, too, have taken the wondrous and have magically made it boring. Fireflies contain reactive phosphor; lightning is just static. Yawn.

I will also admit that Tennyson and I came to accept Brewster's mystical talent far too quickly. Even though I tried to hold on to the wonder, I couldn't. The fact that he could heal—and *steal*—the hurts of others became a commonplace fact. That was my first mistake. Because once you stop marveling at that firefly you caught in a jar, it sits on a shelf with no one to let it out.

38) COTILLION

Before Uncle Hoyt had his steamroller accident and Brew took on the worst beating of his life, I was busy enticing Brewster out of his shell. Tennyson had become his personal trainer; but my role was far more intimate, as well it should be. I was Brew's muse extraordinaire, determined to caress him into a meaningful social life. Having read various books on psychology, I thought I had Brew figured out. All he needed was a little encouragement. Of course I couldn't have been more wrong, but I've never been very good at abandoning theories.

"You need to reinvent yourself," I announced to him at lunch one day, holding his hand across the table for everyone in the cafeteria to see.

"My current invention works just fine," he said. "People stay away from me; I stay away from them."

I shook my head. "Not anymore. You, my sad, poetic stud, are not a loser; and it's time you stopped acting like one. The days of you skulking around the school are over." He tried to eat, but I was holding his eating hand, so all he could do was clumsily stab at the food with a fork in his left fist.

"Maybe I like skulking."

"You'll like having friends more." But he didn't seem convinced, only concerned. "Are you going to look me in the eye and tell me that you don't want friends?" I gave him back his hand, but he didn't switch the fork, leaving his hand available for me to take again. I smiled, marveling at all the little things that mean so much, and wondered when I had become so cloyingly Hallmark.

"It's not that I don't want friends," he said. "I just don't think it's a good idea."

But good idea or not, I was going to make it happen. The next in a long line of Brewster-related missions. As I've said, I'm not the most popular girl in school, but I'm not unpopular either. That makes me socially balanced, which means my friends are balanced, too; and those are the types of people most likely to warm up to Brew. I called over my friend Hannah Garcia, because she can slide a turtle out of its shell without it even knowing.

"Hannah," I said as she sat down with us, "Brewster is under the delusion that he's socially inept."

Brew threw up his hands. "Brontë!"

"Oh, don't get out the heart paddles!" I told him, then turned back to Hannah. "As I was saying, he's been conditioned by circumstance to believe he is not worthy. We need an independent assessment."

"Brontë! You're embarrassing me!" he said.

Hannah waved a hand. "Get over it." Then she studied him honestly and objectively. "Well," she said. "First of all, he's tall. Secondly, he's cute. Third, he's your boyfriend, and you have excellent taste in friends."

"Thank you."

"So," concluded Hannah, "he receives a nine on the acceptability scale."

"Just a nine?" I asked.

"If he was a ten, he'd be going out with me." Then she winked at him and strode away.

Brew was completely red in the face, but he also had the biggest smile I'd ever seen. I took both of his hands across the table, because all eating had stopped anyway. "You know what I think?" I told him. "I think we need to go out one night with a bunch of my friends, introduce you to life as I know it, and have a fantastic time."

"Okay, sure," he said, still pink and as giddy as could be.

I planned the event like it was a major gala. A one-man cotillion, sans tuxedo. It was just a bunch of us going down to the mall for burgers after school on Thursday, but I made sure I invited just the right people—the ones who, like Hannah, would make Brew feel comfortable, even while making him feel uncomfortable. There were six of us all together—not too few, not too many.

"I can't stay long," he said when he arrived, which is what he always said whenever he went anywhere. I leaned forward and kissed him, then moved to whisper in his ear, pausing to steal a whiff of his coconut hair conditioner, which, for some reason I couldn't quite fathom, drove me wild.

"Trust me," I told him, "you won't want to leave."

But that just got him worried.

We all had a great time that night; and although Brew was mostly quiet, he was accepted in a way he'd never been before. Brew was embraced by my friends and was finally able to feel a part of a circle larger than just his immediate family.

As I predicted, he stayed longer than he'd intended to.

"I like your friends," Brew told me as he left. "I didn't think I would, but I like them. A lot."

I went home thinking that I had accomplished something remarkable.

He went home to find his uncle taking out a life's worth of frustrations on his brother.

39) SUBTERFUGE

Grandparents everywhere talk about how they walked five miles to school each day in the snow, barefoot, and chased by wolves; but it's not like that anymore. Most everyone we know drives or gets driven. But Tennyson and I had recently taken to walking to school, even though it's almost a mile. The thing is, if we walked we got out of the house earlier. If we walked we didn't have to sit in a car with Mom and wonder whose awful cologne we were smelling. If we walked we didn't have to sit in a car with Dad, who used to be talkative but now had adopted a code of silence while driving. At least Tennyson and I talked to each other as we walked—even if it was only to argue.

"Dad seemed okay last weekend," Tennyson said as we made our way through a drizzly morning. It was Friday, the day after Brew's big night out with my friends and me, so I was still riding a good mood.

"When?" I asked.

"We were playing basketball. Brew was there."

I thought about it, and wished I could have been there to see Dad being his old self—and to see Brew play ball. His workouts with Tennyson have definitely been defining his body, and, okay, I'll admit I had a primal kind of desire to see those muscles in motion.

"Dad was like his old self," said Tennyson, "but there was something about it . . ."

I didn't know where Tennyson was going with this, and I don't think he knew either, because he never finished the thought.

Up ahead, when we were just a couple of blocks from school, we saw a tall, lumbering form in a leather bomber jacket. He had on a sweatshirt underneath and the hood was over his head, but I didn't have to see his face to know who it was.

"Brew!" I called out.

He turned to look, but just for a second. Then, instead of waiting for us, he picked up his pace.

"Look, he's running away from you!" said Tennyson. "I really like this guy."

I ran to catch up with Brew, both annoyed and confused. For all those big strides, he wasn't moving very fast; and I caught up with him in about a block. I grabbed his arm, and he turned his shoulder away, so I tugged on him harder, until I got a glimpse of his face beneath the hood. What I saw almost made me stumble into traffic.

His lips were swollen, and he had smudges of makeup on his face, clearly trying to conceal a black eye.

"Wh . . . what happened to you?"

He shrugged. "I was having a catch with Cody and missed the ball."

"You're lying!"

He didn't deny it. "So?"

Now I could see that it wasn't just his eye; it was also in the way he held himself, the way he walked—like there wasn't a single part of his body that didn't hurt. I wanted to hold him but was afraid holding him would hurt him, too. "Did your uncle do this to you?"

He stayed quiet for a second and looked toward the school. "No," he said. And then he said, "Yes."

He seemed even more surprised than me that the word *yes* had come out of his mouth. I could tell he had every intention of keeping it secret forever. Suddenly he became pale with very real terror. Fear of me. Fear of me knowing.

I wasn't really prepared for the truth either—I was more stunned by it than anything else. Across the street a few kids laughed. They weren't laughing at us, but still it bothered me. How dare they laugh within a hundred yards of this truth?

"What about Cody?" I asked.

"Cody's fine. He's better than fine."

"You have to tell someone."

"I just told *you*."

"I mean someone important."

"Who? The principal? The police?"

"Yes!"

By now Tennyson had caught up with us and was just staring, stupefied. The bell rang at school, but I didn't care. Lateness was not a concern.

"If I tell anyone, then they'll take us away from my uncle," Brew said. "And things will get a whole lot worse."

"What could possibly be worse than being beaten within an inch of your life?"

He didn't answer me—not verbally—but there was an answer in his eyes that had such a high windchill factor, I actually shivered.

"I can handle it," he said. "I've got it all worked out. In a few months I'll turn sixteen, and I can become an emancipated minor. I'll move out, take Cody with me, and Uncle Hoyt won't be able to stop me."

"That's assuming you're still alive!"

"I'll be fine. But if we get taken away from my uncle now, Cody and I will get put in a home . . . we'll probably get split up. And in a place like that there's no way I can hide what I can do. People will know. And once they know . . ."

Again a blast of those windchill eyes. I wanted to argue him to the ground on this one, but that icy gaze shut me down.

"Who knows," Brew said. "Maybe my uncle will change."

Then Tennyson, who I totally forgot about, chimed in. "Bullies don't change unless they want to," Tennyson said. "Trust me, I know."

We had to go to the authorities. We had to. This was a text-book case of abuse, and turning the man in was the right thing to do—no question. Except that this was Brewster Rawlins. If this were anyone else but Brew, I'd have gone straight to the Powers That Be and ratted out his uncle in an instant; but all the rules of normalcy and right and wrong broke down around Brew. What do you do with a textbook case when no one's written the textbook?

Suddenly I flashed to something I learned in biology. There are some animals that die without explanation if you take them out of their familiar environment. Even if they came from a horrible, hostile environment, they still die.

"You have to trust me," Brew said. "Please . . ."

What could be worse than his uncle? Only Brewster knew the real answer to that. And even though it went against every-thing I knew to be right, I reluctantly entered into his con-spiracy of silence.

And I guess I wasn't the only one.

"You have to come up with a believable story or the teach-ers will be all over you," Tennyson told him. "If anyone asks about your eye, tell them that I beat you up for dating Brontë—and if I have to back it up, I will."

I gaped at Tennyson, unable to believe the suggestion. "No!"

"Well, do you have a better idea?" he snapped.

But I just looked away, because I had nothing but misgivings.

Brew, on the other hand, was genuinely moved by Tennyson's offer. "You'd do that for me?"

And Tennyson said, with his typical smirk, "Sure. What's a friend for if he can't take credit for punching you out?"

Brew took Tennyson up on his offer; and before lunch, people were buzzing with the news that Tennyson had beaten him senseless. My friends came out to console and support me, calling Tennyson every name in the book; and in turn, Tennyson's friends supported him, giving him kudos and high fives that he had to accept or else risk tainting the credibility of Brew's story. Suddenly Tennyson and I were at war with each other in the eyes of our classmates, and no one but Brew knew that it was all fake—a tricky, nasty subterfuge designed at throwing everyone off the track.

I couldn't help but feel I'd made a terrible, terrible mistake. There were so many times during that awful day when I held my phone with 911 dialed in, ready to hit Send, but in the end I didn't do it.

I don't know how things would have been different if I had made that call. Maybe it might have saved Brew from what happened next. On the other hand, it was going to happen one way or another, no matter what any of us did.

BREWSTER

40) EMBOLISM

(I)

Where sorrow waits,
With cold and clammy hands,
Shaking in grim anticipation,
Is where I must return.
Home.
A house in a fallow field,
Losing its battle with time,
The wreck and ruin,
And the man inside,
Who never laid a hand on me,
Yet left me battered.
My uncle.
Nothing ever changes,
But the fear fermenting to dread,
As Cody and I go home.

(II)

"Do ya think he's calmed down?"
"Do ya think he got his job back?"
Do you think, do you think, do you think?
"I don't know, Cody."

What I mean to say is I don't care, because my uncle has cut
my soul from my body, leaving bitterness behind; a
stretch-lipped grimace of futility, because whatever
happens to my uncle happens to me.
Even as his own hope is strangled, so is mine, beaten like a
blunt boot to my ribs, snuffed like a candle with too
short a wick, and not even Brontë can rekindle it.
What he's done is unforgivable.

"Maybe he'll be okay."
"Maybe he'll be sorry, ya think?"
Maybe, maybe, maybe.
"We'll see, Cody."

I creak open the rusty gate—from here it's thirty-eight steps
across the field to our door, steps I take slowly, in no
hurry to know the answers to Cody's questions, when
suddenly a jagged sound peels at the edge of our
awareness, stopping us in our muddy tracks.
"Did you hear that?"

Something has shattered—a tinkling, muffled by closed
     windows—then another smash of a different, finer
     timbre. The first smash was glass, the second china,
     and Cody now looks to me with the wide eyes of fear
     mercifully cushioned by innocence.
          "What's he doing in there, Brew?"
Reaching deeply into my pocket, I scavenge a few crumpled
     bills and hand them to Cody, telling him to go to
     Ben & Jerry's; and, grabbing the bills, he backs away
     from another, louder crash inside.
          "Guess he didn't get his job back."
Cody runs to smother his fear in Cherry Garcia, and I go to
     face my uncle alone.

                              (III)
I'll never understand how a man can live his life
With his finger on the self-destruct button,
Holding it there day after day,
Blinded by an obsession to press it
But lacking the conviction to do even that.
This was my Uncle Hoyt before today,
But today, the auto-destruct sequence is engaged,
And counting down.

My uncle has taken up batting practice with dinnerware.
A minefield of broken china and glass

Litters the floor in every room.
He lobs a gravy boat into the air,
I believe it was once my grandmother's,
Then he swings the Louisville Slugger,
Detonation in blue and white shrapnel.
I can smell scotch everywhere
And wonder how much of that amber poison
Is pickling his brain.
He hurls a teacup, swings, and misses,
Taking out the hanging kitchen lamp instead.
And he mumbles,

"Close enough."

I should turn tail,
I should just let him be,
But if I'll ever make a stand,
It must be here; it must be now,
And though I know I'm not wired for war,
The time has finally come to fight my own nature.
I'm ready for this dance.

(IV)

A swing of the bat, the sound of my voice,
Tentative, timid, a catch in my throat,
I must take command, I must take the lead,

A swing of the bat, a shattering glass.

I move through the madness and reach for the bat,
Wrench it away from his white-knuckled hands,
I toss it behind me and don't miss a beat,
Time for my uncle to learn a new step.

He turns like a scorpion ready to strike,
But his stinger is dull and his venom is weak,
His eyes blaze with anger, his soul burns with bile,
Like the world is to blame for all of his misery.

> *"Go get your brother; we're leaving tonight,*
> *There's more work up north; there's more hope than here,*
> *You'll do what I tell you; you'll do what I say,*
> *You'll go pack your things, 'cause we're leaving right now."*

The room is in ruins, his bridges are burned,
And Cody and I are still chained to his fate,
His life lies in ruins; his life is not mine,
He gave me these shackles, but I can break free.

And I say to him *"No"* with a break in my voice,
"NO!" sounding much more commanding,
> *"We're not going anywhere; neither are you,*
> *You'll back off right now, or you'll feel my hand."*

"So do it," he says with a strange, slanted grin,
I dare you to hit me—go on, take me down!
What are you waiting for? Knock yourself out,
But don't start a fight you can't finish."

A line in the sand, a dare there between us,
My hand is a weapon; my blood's in a boil,
I strain to move mountains; I strain to swing free,
Denying my nature, I raise up my arm.

Let me, for once, be the bruising brutality,
Let me at last be a fist in the face
Of the vicious injustice my brother and I
Have endured at the hands of our uncle.

But my fist is still fixed by invisible shackles,
The mountain won't move; my hand won't swing free,
I cannot deliver; I only receive,
And he gloats at his victory, laughs at my shame.

"You're weak and you're worthless, that's why you need me.
You're helpless and hopeless; your brother's the same
You'll remember how lucky you are that I'm here.
So you'll take what I dish, and you'll like it."

Then he shifts with a slouch and slumps in a chair,

Something is wrong with him, wrong with me, too,
I can't feel my arm, and I can't move my shoulder,
Feet start to tingle, and skin starts to itch,

My hand's still a fist that I cannot unravel,
My face has gone loose, like an avalanche slide,
My tongue becomes rubber; my lungs barely breathe,
I fall to the ground as my left leg gives way,

And there in the chair Uncle Hoyt is the same,
Our eyes are now locked in a clear understanding,
What falls on my uncle rebounds out to me,
Oh, my God—he's having a stroke!

(V)

"TakeItAway, TakeItAwayFromMeBoy, ThasWhyYerrHere,
IKnowThatNow . . . ThasWhy Y'Came SssoManyYearsAgo,
WhyYerMomDid WhutSheDid . . . NowYerr MySssecondLife,
MySssecondShance, SssecondShance TahMakeSssomething
A Mysself, TahDoItRight, NoMore YearssA LivinOn TheEdge
A MyOwnLoussyLife, NeverNothin More AnClosedDoorss
An MishedOpportunitiess . . . ButYerrChanginThat, you're
ChanginThat RightNowFerMe, Brewshter, you're Makin'
It all all right, My BrokenSpiritBecomin' yours, My
SsorryBodyBecoming yours, I CanFeel it happening,
FeelinBetter, TalkinBetter . . . SpongeItAll away, boy,

'CauseYouCareAbout me, YouCare and can't deny it, I KnowIt
In MyHeart, you KnowIt In yourss, all these YearssA Putting a
roof OverYer head, food in yer stomach, have all GottaCount
for ssomething, not perfect, no, NeverPerfect, but a family,
RealAndTrue, lookin' out ForOneAnother like you're lookin'
out for MeRightNow, and so what if I GetFoul from time to time,
who don't, ButYouCan forgive it right, becausse you understand,
YouCare, and I'm grateful for it, Brew . . . grateful 'cause today
you KnowYourPlace on this good earth . . . your place and
YourPurpose, and that's to ssave me, YourPoorOld Uncle Hoyt,
I can feel it all DrainingAway, the numbness, the heaviness . . .
steal it all away, Yeah, That'sIt . . . and I won't forget it, Brew, and
I'll GiveYou the biggesst shiny marble headsstone and Cody and
I will visit WhenWe can, and flowerss on your birthday, and the
doors of heaven, they're flung OpenWide for you 'cause of what
you're doing today, so take it away, take it away from me, Brew,
like you're supposed to . . . that's why you're here."

(VI)

*I try to speak but my tongue is now fat and lazy, and life
starts trailing away, my body giving in. . . . This can't be
my purpose—to die in my uncle's place, my flesh shutting
down, left leg, left arm, half of me gone, and the other half
beginning to follow, a catastrophic collapse, because I care
just enough to be trapped—and the thought of him walking
out of here free and clear is too much for me to bear—I do not*

want this—I want MY life, not HIS death, and my only hope
is to stop caring—to kill in the depth of my own soul the pity
and compassion I feel for the man who raised me for half my
life—can I do that to you, Uncle Hoyt, now, when it's either
you or me? Can I find it in my heart to NOT find it in my
heart? I dig down, down, down, to make the numbness taking
root in my body invade that place in me that still cares about
you and purge it so that I can leave you—not love, not hate,
but leave you dark and indifferent, in an Arctic cold—I don't
care about you, not now, not anymore . . . and now . . .
and now . . . I can slowly feel sensation coming back to my
face—I don't care what happens to you, Uncle Hoyt—I can
twitch my legs now—and as your fate sinks back into you,
you reach out to grab me— but with my one good hand I do
what I could not do before—I swing my fist and connect with
your jaw, and you fall away—I see your face—how it's losing
muscle tone as the stroke returns to you, sinking in—a mud
slide seeking low ground—I have both my arms back—my
legs are still not strong enough to carry me, but I scramble for
the door on all fours as you wail incomprehensible fury—your
fate is your own again—and if I can get far enough away
and keep myself from caring just long enough, your fate will
stay bound to you—so I drag myself out the door, falling off
the porch, dredging through the mud, still unable to stand,
but the farther away I get, the easier it is, until I can rise to
my feet, until I am at the edge of the range of my gift—until

I can't feel you anymore, Uncle Hoyt, no, I can't feel you at all. I can walk now—with a limp, but I can walk, and I stride powerfully across the field toward the gate. Your death is yours alone, Uncle Hoyt; it's what you created, what you've earned. And you'll know soon enough if God truly has mercy enough to forgive you. Because I can't.

(VII)

I look for Cody,
One foot almost dragging,
And as I cross into a parking lot,
I have to squint from the neon glare of the strip mall,
And yet I'm relieved to be doused with light.
In the ice-cream shop,
Cody stirs a molten mess the color of a storm,
Watching as I make an emergency call
On a borrowed cell phone,
Then says nothing as we leave the shop,
Nothing as we turn toward home,
Nothing, even as distant sirens draw closer.

> *"Hold my hand, Cody."*
>
> *"I'm not a baby."*
>
> *"I said, hold my hand!"*

Because it's not just for him.
It's for me.

(VIII)

Cody and I go home,
With fear fermenting to dread,
For everything has changed.
My uncle.
Who left me battered
Yet never laid a hand on me,
The man inside,
A wreck and ruin,
Losing his battle with time,
In that house in a fallow field.
Home.
Where I must return
Shaking in grim anticipation
With cold and clammy hands
Where death waits.

TENNYSON

41) INCOMMUNICADO

There's no funeral for Uncle Hoyt.

Instead, his ex-wife has him quietly cremated and the ashes shipped back to her in Atlanta, where she will do whatever angry women do with their ex-husband's ashes. Even so, the guy has it easier than Brewster, who has to suffer through The Week From Hell.

FRIDAY: Uncle Hoyt dies under mysterious circumstances.

SATURDAY: There's no word from Brewster, and all we get are rumors from neighborhood kids—not just rumors about how it happened, but where Brew and Cody are now. Brontë and I are completely out of the loop, and it drives us nuts. There's not a single reliable source of information, and all the possibilities are as nerve-racking as SAT choices:

A) "I hear the Bruiser shot his uncle and ran away."

B) "I hear the Bruiser strangled his uncle, and the FBI is holding him."

C) "I hear his uncle was whacked by the Mafia, and now the Bruiser's in the witness protection program."

D) "I hear Bruiser never actually had an uncle, and Ralphy Sherman says they found radioactive material in the basement."

We're the only ones who know Brew well enough to know the answer is E) None of the above.

SUNDAY: Brontë, who has never thrown a punch in her life at anyone but me, gets into a death match cat fight in the street with some cheerleader who calls Brewster a psycho. The offending young lady won't be shaking her pom-poms anytime soon.

"Welcome to the Dark Side," I tell Brontë. She is not amused.

MONDAY: In school, word comes down that Uncle Hoyt's autopsy revealed a blood clot in the brain. It was a stroke, but it's too late to shut down the rumors and the mindless whispers by asinine students that it's just a cover story and that Brewster killed him. We still don't hear from Brewster.

TUESDAY: Brontë accosts our school psychologist—a tall, slithery man who, in my opinion, doesn't exactly engender an air of safety and trust. He claims doctor/patient confidentiality and won't say much of anything at first—but Brontë has a way of charming snakes.

She seems much more relaxed after she finally breaks through to some actual facts. Brew and Cody were taken in by Mrs. Gorton—Cody's old kindergarten teacher, now retired. She lives near Brew's house, saw the police at their place, and took them to her house when social services didn't show.

It was a full day before a social worker even arrived at their door.

WEDNESDAY: We finally receive a call from Brew and get a clearer picture. Apparently, Mr. and Mrs. Gorton are very big in their church, which means setting an example as Pillars of Virtue and doing the whole What Would Jesus Do? thing. Of course, the problem with *them* being an example is that Brewster and Cody have to be examples, too: living testimonies to the grace of God. Brew's the last person to want that kind of spotlight.

"It's much too Huckleberry Finn-ish for me," Brontë says after she gets off the phone with him. "They're keeping Brew and Cody under lock and key as they try to 'civilize' them. They wouldn't even let Brew call me until today. Even in jail they give a person one phone call, don't they?"

I suspect that Brew has other reasons for going incommunicado, but I keep my suspicions to myself.

THURSDAY: Brew still hasn't resurfaced at school, and there's no indication when, or even *if*, he ever will. Perhaps they're transferring Brew and Cody to someplace else.

That afternoon Brontë pays a visit to the Gortons with me in tow for moral support.

"Brewster and Cody aren't at home," Mrs. Gorton says when she answers the door; but her story doesn't wash, because Cody runs out and nearly tackles Brontë with a hug.

"Brewster's sleeping," Mrs. Gorton says—but I see him peeking out between the upstairs blinds then ducking back out of sight. For a Pillar of Virtue, Mrs. Gorton sure does lie a lot. She tells us that the boys have been seeing doctors for much of the week, apparently for both physical and psychological assessments. Considering Brewster's various contusions, which were clearly gifts from their late uncle, many doctors were in order.

"I just want to talk to him," Brontë pleads.

"He doesn't want to see anyone now." This time she's telling the truth—and Brontë knows it, too, because I can see how hurt she is by it.

"Give him this, please," she says. "Tell him it's from Brontë." Then she hands Mrs. Gorton one of those little pastel-colored volumes of bad inspirational poetry—the kind they sell in greeting card stores—definitely not the kind of poetry that Brewster likes; but the woman takes one look at the flowery book and is almost moved to tears.

"Of course I'll give it to him, dear."

We walk home, mission failed.

"Do you really think he'll like those cheesy poems?" I ask.

"It wasn't for him; it was for her," Brontë explains. "To win her over so the next time I come by she'll let me in."

I stand corrected: Mission accomplished.

FRIDAY: Brontë's investigative eavesdropping into teachers' private conversations reveals a problem: In a situation like this, social services bends over backward to make it easy to become a foster parent—basically, anyone without a criminal record can get approved—and since the Gortons had already taken in Brew and Cody, they were being put on the fast track to foster parenthood. However, Mr. Gorton, in his youth, did six months for auto theft before he found religion; and although his criminal history was history and God stuck like glue, it didn't matter. The couple came up short in the eyes of the law.

Now it's only a matter of time before their application is denied. Then Brewster and Cody will be pulled out of the Gortons' home and taken to a state facility, where love and concern get divided like cake at a wedding.

42) DICKENSIAN

That weekend Brontë comes up with the Big Idea. I knew it was coming.

It's Sunday, and we're out front washing Mom's car. It looks like it's about to rain, but it's something to get us out of the house. Something to keep our minds and hands occupied—because you know what they say about idle hands and all. We soap up the car, not even paying attention to the fact that one of the windows is open and we're getting the upholstery wet. Mom won't yell at us about it. She doesn't yell at us much since she's afraid we'll yell back—and lately we have much more powerful ammunition than she does. It's a clear indication that Brontë and I are now the superpowers within our own family, and you don't attack a superpower. Frankly, though, I'd much prefer to have stability return to the region.

"You know what will happen to them once the Gortons get

denied," Brontë says. "They'll end up in some orphanage or workhouse or something."

"Don't be Dickensian," I tell her. "They don't have workhouses in this day and age"—although I'm not quite sure what modern, twenty-first-century orphanages are like. All I know is that once a month there's a big shocking-pink plastic bag around our doorknob screaming for clothes donations for *"the something home for something-something children."* I also know that Brewster's terrified of being sent to one.

"Wherever they end up, it won't be good," she says, wringing out her sponge like she's trying to strangle it.

I know exactly where she's going with this—like I said, I've been waiting for it—but I don't want to deny her the satisfaction of getting there, so I play dumb. "Maybe they'll get other foster parents," I suggest.

"The last thing Brewster and Cody need is to be handed off over and over again." She soaps up the hood of the car in serpentine curves as she wends her way to her point. "It just seems so ridiculous," she says, "when we have a spare room big enough for both of them."

I sponge the back window in small, even circles, taking my time before feeding her the line she already knows is coming. "Dad's living in the spare room."

She shrugs. "So what? It won't be forever."

I don't comment on that, because the future can hold many things when it comes to our father's sleeping arrangements.

He could move back into the master bedroom with Mom; he could move out; he could pitch a tent in the backyard—the roulette wheel is still spinning and there's no telling if Dad, God rest his soul, will land on a black or a red number.

"Even if we could give them the spare room," I tell her, "do you really think Mom and Dad would allow you and your boyfriend to live under the same roof?"

"They're very progressive," Brontë counters, "and besides, we're not sexually active, thank you very much."

I smirk. "You say that now."

She hurls her sponge at me. I duck and it hits the mailbox.

"Forget it," she says, exasperated. "Forget I said anything. It was a dumb idea anyway."

But she's wrong about that, and I think about that day playing basketball—and how good both Dad and I felt with Brew in the mix, changing the whole family dynamic. Maybe what our little roulette wheel needs isn't black or red but a nice dose of double-zero green.

I retrieve my sister's sponge and hand it back to her. "I'll have to be the one to suggest it," I say, "because if it comes from you, no matter how progressive they are, they'll freak out."

"No, forget it; with everything that's going on between Mom and Dad, the last thing they need is two kids with issues in the house."

I smirk again. "Don't you mean four?"

She sneers but holds on to her sponge, having deemed my comment not sponge worthy. "Actually six," she says, "if you include Mom and Dad."

I hose off the suds and hand her a towel for drying. "Leave it to me," I tell her, because although I don't often mess with Mom's and Dad's heads, when I do, I'm pretty good at it.

43) AUDACIOUS

Dad's in the spare bedroom grading papers on Emerson. Mom is out, probably with the Ewok. They're rarely home at the same time except in the evenings. The first things I notice when I enter the room are the suitcases. Two of them. They've migrated from the basement. A pair of no-nonsense gray roll-aboards made of sturdy ballistic nylon. They can catch a bullet, and your suit would still stay pressed.

The cases are not being packed; but they sit ominously in the corner, waiting for the day, the hour, the moment when Dad will use them and move out. I try not to think about them as I approach my father.

"Papers from your grad students?" I ask him.

"Yes," he says, "although to read these essays, you'd never know."

Looking at the essays, I can see handwritten notes between

every line. You could create a whole second essay from what he's written back to them.

"Busywork," I say.

"Excuse me?"

"You're filling the hours with busywork so you don't have to think about stuff with Mom. I get it."

He rubs his forehead like Advil is in order. "Is there something you want, Tennyson?"

I pick up one of the essays and casually pretend to read it. "I guess everything's relative," I say. "I mean, what's going on in our family is nothing compared to what happened to Brewster Rawlins. What's happening to him, I mean."

Dad continues red-inking his students' work. "Sometimes you have to count your blessings."

"Brontë's all broken up over it."

Finally Dad puts down the paper he's reading. "Are they still dating?"

It surprises me that he doesn't know that; but then, these days nothing should surprise me. Rather than make assumptions about how much he knows, I bring him up to date—the fact that Brew and his brother have no family and that Mr. Gorton's ancient criminal record leaves everyone royally screwed. I don't tell him about the healing thing because I'm not an idiot.

Once I'm done with the saga of woe, Dad throws me a glance—I think by now he knows what's coming—then he returns to his work. "Too bad we can't help," he says.

"Actually, we can."

"Absolutely not!"

This was okay; I was expecting this. Walls don't fall without effort.

"We're in no position to take them in," he says. "Besides, someone else will; and if not, well, I'm sure social services will take fine care of them."

"Do you really believe that?"

Dad sighs. "Are you completely clueless, Tennyson? Do you have any idea how bad the timing is? Do you even see what's going on between your mother and me?"

"I see everything," I tell him coldly. "I see more than you." And I believe that's true.

"So then, case closed."

That expression "case closed" makes me look over at the two suitcases standing against the wall like a pair of hollow tombstones.

"Maybe taking them in will change things," I suggest to my father. "What if putting ourselves out for someone else is just what we all need? What you and Mom need . . ."

Dad sighs. "Putting ourselves out for someone else? Now you sound like your sister."

"Then you'd better listen, because me sounding like Brontë is one of the signs of the apocalypse—and if the end of the world is coming, good deeds could earn you Judgment Day brownie points."

He doesn't laugh. His shoulders are still slumped; his attitude has not changed. "It's a nice idea, but we can't do it. Now, please—I really have a lot of work to do."

I sit there a moment more, pretending to weigh the validity of the things he's said. I pretend like I'm getting a clue.

"You're right," I tell him. "I'm sorry I bothered you." I shift in my chair as if I'm getting ready to stand up and leave. Then I say, "Mom would never allow it anyway."

I can practically hear the hairs on his neck bristling. "Then for once your mother and I would be in agreement."

"Well, yeah . . . ," I say. "But even if you wanted to take them in, she'd shut it down."

He still won't look at me. "It's not like your mother makes all the decisions around here."

"No?"

He taps his red pen on his stack of essays. Finally he turns to look at me. "You think I don't know what you're doing?"

"What am I doing?"

"You're trying to manipulate me into taking in Brewster and his brother."

I don't deny it. "Is it working?" I ask.

He laughs at that. Now all bets are off. I don't know how this is going to play out. Then Dad says, "If you want it to work, you need to make me think it's *my* idea."

"It *was* your idea," I say in total deadpan seriousness. "You suggested it just a second ago."

He laughs again. "My mistake." And he shakes his head at my bald-faced audacity. He thinks about it for a moment, or pretends to think about it—I don't know who's toying with whom anymore. Then he says, "I'll discuss it with your mother, and we'll make a *joint* decision."

"That's all I can ask," I say, "that you and Mom give serious thought to a decision that Brontë and I will remember for the rest of our lives."

He studies me with that tentative gaze of parental evaluation—you know the one: It's both a little bit proud and a little bit frightened at the same time. Then he says, *"So shines a good deed in a weary world."*

I know this one! I snap my fingers and say, "Shakespeare— *The Merchant of Venice.*"

"Actually," says my father, "I was thinking Gene Wilder as Willy Wonka, but both answers, A and B, are valid."

Mom and Dad have their discussion, and the answer is still no. The Gortons are denied foster-parent status less than a week later; and as soon as social services can wade through their own paperwork, Brew and Cody will be sent to *"the something home for something-something children,"* vanishing into the system, never to be seen again.

If the wall Mom and Dad have erected is going to fall, it has to fall soon. It's Brontë who completes the erosion process, turning herself into a human tsunami, as if it's a secret superpower. Although I'll never admit it to her, I'm in awe, and a little bit frightened of her now.

I'm there when Jericho falls. It begins with a phone call, which I'm about to pick up; but Brontë, seeing the number on the caller ID, stops me. It rings one more time, and I hear Mom take the call in the hallway. We both listen.

"Excuse me, you're from *whose* office?" we hear Mom say. "An attorney? What's this all about?"

I don't like the sound of that. When your parents are living on a fraying tightrope, a call from a lawyer is a very bad sign. I turn to Brontë, but the look on her face is more anticipation than dread.

"Let me get this straight—you're calling for Brontë? Why would you want to speak to my daughter?" Mom listens for a moment more, then Brontë whispers to me: "They won't tell her a thing—attorney/client confidentiality."

"You hired a lawyer?"

"Consulted," Brontë tells me. "Consultations are free."

The phone call ends abruptly with Mom saying, "No, wait, don't hang up," which they obviously do.

Since no one in our family sits down for dinner together anymore, Brontë makes a point of eating with Mom. I join them because I love a good fireworks display. But instead it's painfully quiet until Mom says, "Brontë, there's something I want to talk to you about."

I know that Mom means to broach the topic of the phone

call, but instead Brontë blindsides Mom with something else.

"I've decided to quit the swim team."

"That's not what I . . . what?"

"I've decided I need to get a job instead. I've been told that self-sufficiency is the first step."

Mom's still mentally backpedaling, trying to catch a gear. "First step toward what?"

"To becoming an emancipated minor."

Mom takes a deep breath and lets it out, the dots finally connecting in her head. The fact that Brontë actually called a lawyer makes it hit exceptionally hard. "And why would you want that?" she says, trying to sound bright and unbothered by it.

"Well, you have to admit that you and Dad have not exactly been warm and nurturing lately. And the fact that you won't consider helping Brewster and Cody makes it very clear this is not a place I want to be."

Then Mom looks Brontë in the eye with the cold gaze of a serious parental warning. "Listen to me, because I will only say this once, Brontë," she says. "I will not be blackmailed by you."

Brontë holds the gaze, and strikes back with equal force behind her words. "Actions have consequences, Mom. You taught me that. Your actions are no exception."

Then she gets up and strides out of the kitchen.

Now I'm alone with Mom, who's no longer eating. "Wow," I say; and since I really am blown away by what Brontë has just done, I say "Wow" again, truly speechless.

That night I ask Brontë if she really means it. She seems terrified by the question.

"I don't make idle threats," she says—and I suddenly realize that she's not scared of our parents' response; she's scared of her own determination, because if Mom and Dad don't do something for Brew and Cody, she *will* quit the swim team, she *will* get a job, and eventually maybe she *will* go all the way with her threat to become emancipated.

I want to comfort her somehow; but again, all I can say is "Wow."

Nothing more is said about it until the following day, but then Dad tells Brontë and me that he and Mom are "open to considering the possibility of maybe temporarily helping Brew and Cody if no one else steps forward."

They schedule an appointment with the social worker, who comes by our house the same day. I suppose she's trying to make up for botching things the day Uncle Hoyt died. She must have sold used cars in a previous life, because although Mom and Dad keep insisting all they want is information, the appointment ends with an application, fingerprinting, and a background check. "So you'll already be approved as foster parents should you decide to move forward," the social worker says; but I think our parents know full well that there's no closing this door once it's open.

"God bless you," the social worker tells them. "God bless you both."

Then Brontë smothers Mom and Dad in kisses in a way she hasn't done since we were little. "I love you both so, so much!" she tells them. "I knew you would do the right thing."

Our phone rings a week later. Sometimes when the call is momentous enough, you know exactly who's calling and why even before you pick up the phone. I've never been one to believe in that kind of intuition, but lately I've had to broaden my mind to a whole range of things I used to dismiss. When that phone rings, I know just as certainly as I know my own name what the call is about even before Dad says, "Hello?"

44) CATHARTIC

The Gortons drive Brew and Cody over early on Wednesday evening. Mrs. Gorton is all teary-eyed as she hugs Cody, as if she's either sending him off to summer camp or handing him over to agents of Satan.

They chat with my parents briefly. Brew shakes my parents' hands tentatively as they welcome him. Cody doesn't bother with such formalities; he's already raced in and has made himself at home. All the while I notice the Gortons never make eye contact with Brewster; and when they tell him good-bye, there's a chilly formality to it, like they'd rather not say anything to him at all. They hurry to their car, they drive off, and there it is: Brewster Rawlins, creepy dude deluxe, is now my foster brother.

This is the first time we're seeing Brew face-to-face since his uncle died. Not a big deal for me, but I know it's a big deal for my sister. He stands at the threshold sheepishly, holding a small suitcase that contains all the worldly possessions he chose to salvage from the farmhouse. He faces Brontë in our foyer in a guarded standoff in which nothing much is said.

"Hi."

"Hi."

"You okay?"

"Yeah, you?"

"Yeah."

Walking on eggshells cannot begin to describe the moment—and the dinner that follows is the very definition of discomfort . . . or at least it starts that way.

The mood is set right away by Cody, who can't stop talking about how they found Uncle Hoyt. "He was all pale, like the blood been sucked outta him." To hear him tell it, you'd think the man got attacked by a chupacabra—and I'm sure the story gets wilder every time he tells it. By now Cody has had a haircut, compliments of the Gortons, and he looks semicivilized. Still, he keeps shaking his head like he's trying to fling hair out of his face. That habit's not going to go away for a good while.

"And his eyes," says Cody, "they was open and all bulgy, like he saw a ghost!"

"It's very sad," Brontë says. "Would anyone like some milk?"

"Did you hear everything in the house was all broke up?" Cody says. "Nothing left—like he blew it apart with his *mind* before he died!"

"That's enough, Cody," Brewster says under his breath; but my mom gently pats Cody's hand.

"Talk about it all you want, Cody," she tells him. "It's very cathartic to talk it out."

I can see Cody mouthing the word *cathartic* with a grimace, like it's a verbal Brussels sprout; and I wonder if our parents are going to inflict him and Brew with a daily power word, too.

If nothing else, this has forced Mom and Dad to sit at the same dinner table again—and Mom has actually cooked a meal. Okay, so it's lasagna from Costco, but at least she turned on the oven and put it in!

"I know you've had a rough time of it," Mom says, mostly to Brew, "but from here on in, you don't have to worry about anything."

"More lasagna?" says Brontë. I think she believes that if everyone's mouth can be kept full, there's less chance that someone will say something unfortunate.

"How's your basketball coming?" Dad asks Brew.

"Haven't played since that time with you guys."

"Well, we'll have to do it again."

It's as if our parents have begun a new competition to see who can be more compassionate to troubled youth.

"I hope you boys are okay with the guest room," Mom says.

And I say, "So, where will you sleep, Dad?"

I just meant it as a simple question, but then realize that this is one of those unfortunate moments Brontë has been trying to avoid. I shove some lasagna in my mouth, but it's too late. I glance to Mom, who fusses with her napkin rather than look at me. The fact that no one has discussed with Brontë and me how this is all going to work is yet another symptom of the downed communications line within our family.

"Well, Tennyson," says my father, "I suppose I could room with you. . . ." He tries to be flip and funny when he says it, but he can't mask the tension thundering in just behind his words.

"Sure, whatever," I say. I think this is the first time in years I've used the expression "whatever," as it's on our family's list of banned slang; but when I say it, there's an audible breath of relief from both of my parents.

Then Brontë says, "You and Mom have shared a bed for seventeen years; I don't think it'll kill you to share it a little while longer."

He takes a few moments to chew, and then Dad says, "True." I can sense no emotion in his response either way.

Brontë, who was so determined to shut everyone else up just a minute ago, is still not done. "I mean, we have a situation, and we should all make the best of it; isn't that right, Mom?"

"We'll work things out to the best of our ability," my mother says. She really should run for Congress.

"Now, you know this isn't permanent," Dad reminds us all.

"Yes, sir," says Brew.

"But we are more than happy to have you here for as long as it takes," Mom adds.

"Yes, ma'am," says Brew. No one in memory has ever called my parents *sir* or *ma'am*.

"I'm sure they'll find a more appropriate family who'd be willing to take both of you in."

"And," adds Dad, "who aren't quite as strange as us."

"Don't worry," Brew says, looking over at Brontë with a grin. "I like strange."

She gives him a playful love-hit, which sends Dad to prickly, uncomfortable places. "The guest room has its own bathroom," Dad says. "It's convenient—you'll never need to go upstairs."

Brontë drops her fork on her plate for effect. "My God, Dad, why don't you install motion sensors on the stairs to make sure he doesn't come up at night?"

"Don't think we haven't thought of that, dear," says Mom in her I-can-be-as-impertinent-as-you voice, and for a moment—just the slightest moment—things feel almost normal.

45) PALPABLE

An hour after dinner, I can hear Mom and Dad in their bedroom discussing Cody-and-Brew-related details.

Their bedroom.

I like the fact that I can say that again. This is the most Mom and Dad have said to each other in weeks. It must be a relief to have someone else's crisis to take the place of their own. I suppose surrogate stress is a kinder, gentler form of trauma. As I listen to their muffled voices, I feel confident that things will be okay. Brew and Cody have been here for just a couple of hours and already their presence is making a difference. I can only hope that those good feelings stay.

Cody has already taken root in the family room and plays video games. Mom removed all games that remotely suggest violence and death—but Cody's doing a good job of making harmless cartoon characters suffer in fresh and inventive ways.

"This game sucks," he says, "but I like it."

Brontë's in the spare room, which I guess isn't spare any-more, talking to Brew in hushed tones. They stop the moment I enter.

"I was just briefing Brew on the state of the union," Brontë informs me.

"As in the nation?"

"As in our parents."

"I'm sure he can see it for himself."

There's an unrest in Brew's face that borders on sheer ter-ror, so palpable I can almost feel it like heat from a furnace. It stands in stark contrast to my own growing sense of well-being. I wonder if Brontë sees it too or if she's just so happy he's here, she can't see how it's affecting him. The question is *why*? What is he so worried about?

"I'd better go," Brontë says, "before Dad finds me in here and decides to lock me away in a tower." She gives Brew a quick kiss and leaves. I don't think she ever notices just how deep his fear goes.

"Do you think she's still mad at me for not calling her right away?"

I think about how to best answer him. "She wasn't mad," I say. "Just worried."

"I didn't mean to worry her."

I put up my hand to stop him before he launches into an apology. "I'm sure Brontë understands, but she's a chronic fixer. She freaks out if she's not allowed to repair a situation."

"She couldn't fix this."

"Actually, she did," I remind him. "I mean, you're here, aren't you?"

Then Brew looks down, nervously picking at his finger-nails, and asks the million-dollar question. "Do your parents know about . . . about the *stuff* I do?"

I shake my head. "No—and unless they start smacking each other with two-by-fours, I don't think they'll find out."

"But if they get a bad cut, and it suddenly goes away . . ."

"Let's hope they don't," I tell him.

He unpacks his bag slowly and methodically. "People in school are talking about what happened, aren't they?"

I know he's worried about going back to school. I'm about to tell him that there's no problem; but I don't want to lie to him, so I just shrug like I have nothing to say.

"They think I killed him, don't they?"

I can't escape the question, so I tell him the truth as tact-fully as I can. "There are some imbeciles who have come up with their own version of how your uncle died," I say; "but most people aren't that stupid. Still, they might be a little standoffish."

"I'm used to that." He crosses the room to put some clothes in the dresser, and I notice he's limping. In fact, he'd been favoring his right foot ever since he arrived. It's different from the limp he had when he took Brontë's sprained ankle.

I wonder what that's all about, but I don't want to ask.

He looks into the open drawer for a moment, his thoughts elsewhere. "Tennyson . . . ," he says, ". . . I didn't kill my uncle." And I can see how desperate he is for me to believe it.

"I never thought you did."

Yet he doesn't seem relieved. Maybe that's because I'm not the one he's trying to convince. As the conversation is headed toward dangerous rapids, I make a quick course correction.

"So . . . how were the Gortons?"

"I didn't like them," Brew says.

"Yeah, they did seem a bit cold. . . ."

Brew closes the dresser drawer. "No—I mean I *couldn't* like them. Because if I did, I'd have osteoporosis, arthritis, varicose veins, and who knows what else."

It takes me a moment to understand what he's saying, then the truth dawns on me. If he had liked them, he'd have ended up taking on all of their infirmities—even the ones he didn't know about.

"I had to do stuff to make them hate me right away," Brew says. "Steal things, break things on purpose. It was easier to dislike them if they didn't like me first."

"Sort of a preemptive strike," I say. Only now do I begin to really understand how difficult it must be to carry the weight of his strange ability. He has to live his life in an emotional bubble—never caring—or he'd never survive. It's a huge deal that he's let Brontë and me into that bubble. I think back to the very first time he shook my hand—how he hesitated as we stood there in his kitchen. I had no idea what a huge decision he was making at that moment.

"Well, don't start breaking stuff around here," I tell him, "or you and I are gonna have to revisit that black eye."

"I won't," he says.

"I mean . . you do like our family, right?"

He hesitates—just as he did that time he shook my hand. I feel like the fate of the world is resting on his answer, and I don't know why.

"Yes," he finally says. "Yes, I do."

46) SUBCUTANEOUS

"Is it true? Because I won't believe it unless I hear it from your mouth—did the Bruiser *actually* move in with you?"

"Yeah," I tell Katrina. "Him and his brother."

It's lunchtime on Monday—Brew's first day back at school. Katrina sits across the table from me, gaping like she might expel the salad she just ate. "That's just insane!"

"It wasn't my idea," I tell her, and get mad at myself for lying. Why do I feel I have to lie to her about it?

"Well, I hope you lock your door at night, because I don't want to be interviewed on CNN or something about how my boyfriend was murdered in his sleep."

I squirm on the bench, feeling like I've developed a nest of ants under my skin; but it's just Katrina. "Leave the guy alone," I say; "he's not so terrible."

"No? Well, Ozzy O'Dell says—"

"I don't care what Ozzy O'Dell says; he's a moron."

Katrina's speechless, like she's the one I just insulted. "I'm sorry," she says, finally realizing that Bruiser-bashing is not a sport I engage in anymore. "If it'll make you happy, I'll tell everyone what a perfectly, wonderfully normal guy the Bruiser is."

I wonder if she even remembers his actual name. Did I know his name before Brontë started dating him? "You don't have to do that either," I mumble.

She cocks her head and studies me, screwing up her lips. "Listen, I know what you're going through. When *my* parents got divorced, I was all stressed-out, too."

"My parents are *not* getting divorced."

"Divorced, separated, whatever—the point is, temporary insanity goes with the territory, so I understand why you're so snippy, and it's okay."

Hearing that just makes me feel more "snippy," because maybe she's partly right. But on the other hand, my parents have stopped fighting, and there's a sense of balance returning to the house. Well, maybe not balance, but a kind of cushioning—like we're all inside a big bounce house, and no matter how hard we hit the wall, we'll just rebound.

"I'm fine with my parents," I tell her. "And they're fine, too."

She sighs. "Denial is normal. You'll get over it." She gives me a slim grin and a knowing nod, then says, "So, are we studying tonight?"

"Not tonight," I tell her. "I've got too many things going on at home." Which is true on one level and false on another. I don't have anything specifically that I have to do; but lately I've been feeling more and more like a homebod—not wanting to go out—and when I am out, I want to get home as quickly as possible. Maybe Katrina's right. Maybe the turmoil in my family is affecting me. All I know is that, in spite of it, when I'm home I feel safe, like nothing can hurt me.

47) DECIMATING

Once in a while our school has half days, and the teachers spend the afternoon "in service," which I think must be group therapy for having to deal with us. On those days a bunch of us usually go to the shopping center across the street. We hang out at the Burger King, or Ahab's Coffee, or the smoothie place, depending on the length of the line.

Usually my friends are pretty cool, except, of course, when they're not. And it's not only my friends that I hang out with, because they have friends, too, not all of whom I like. But as is the way with these things, you tolerate the bozos your friends bring to the table.

So, I'm sitting in the smoothie place with the usual suspects, drinking smoothies and munching on chips, when in walks Brewster, who gets in line—only I don't see him first; my friend Joe Crippendorf does. Crippendorf looks at me and says under his breath, "Guess they'll serve anyone in here."

It gets several snickers from around the table. I take a long suck on my smoothie and say to Crippendorf, also beneath my breath, "Uncalled for."

He gets the message right away, and he's wise enough to stop. However, one of the bozos my friends have brought along today is Ozzy O'Dell, the hairless wonder, who takes it upon himself to pick up where Crippendorf left off.

"He's here because they've got a new flavor," Ozzy says. "Citrus Psycho." A few of the same characters laugh, which just encourages him. "Yeah," Ozzy continues, "it's full of fruits and nuts."

Crippendorf tells Ozzy he's a moron, and it's seconded by a couple of others; but there are still a few who are laughing.

"I'd shut it if I were you," I warn him.

But Ozzy thinks he's on a roll. He goes right over to Brew. "So, Bruiser, how is it you're back at school and not in jail for what you did? You must have a good lawyer."

Now only two kids give the slightest chuckle—the rest realize that Ozzy has crossed the line; but Ozzy's the kind of cretin who needs only one person's laughter to sustain his stupidity—his own.

I stand up. "O'Dell, why don't you sit your waxed ass down and leave him alone."

"Oh, sorry," he taunts, "I forgot you two are like brothers now, right? Or is it sisters?"

Now everyone's looking at me and making that low *ooooooh* sound that precedes most high school confrontations.

"Are you gonna let him get away with that?" says Crippendorf, because your friends just love to stir the water when they smell blood.

I keep my cool; but when I see the look on Brew's face, I know I must retaliate. I grab Ozzy's smoothie, which he left on the table, and take a long sip—gurgling it in my mouth—and I say, with my mouth bubbling with smoothie, "Is it my imagination or is this smoothie saliva flavored?" Then I put the straw back in my mouth and backwash every last bit down the straw and into the cup, along with some potato chip bits that were still in my mouth.

Even Brew grins at that—but Ozzy sees the grin and goes after him. "What are *you* smiling at?" He pushes Brew against a glass display case, which rattles loudly enough to draw the manager's attention.

"Hey!" yells the manager. "Take it outside!"

Ozzy turns to me, getting all red—not just on his face but on top of his shaved head as well. "You're buying me a new one!" he demands.

But we both know that that's not gonna happen, so he steps forward and pushes me.

I only remember fighting Ozzy O'Dell once. It was back in second grade. He threw these weird windmill-like punches, which was probably an early sign that the swim team was in his future.

"Outside," the manager says, "or I call the cops!" Apparently he doesn't care how much blood is spilled as long as it's not on his property.

I storm outside, and Ozzy's right behind me, along with everyone else.

I probably look pretty angry, but actually I'm not. It's weird. All I feel is a desire to end this and get on with my day—but when I glance over at Brew, he's clenching his fists and gritting his teeth. He's got enough anger for both of us. I know that it's my responsibility to shut Ozzy up, because if I don't, it'll never end. He'll go on tormenting Brew, spreading lies, and making the Bruiser's life miserable.

I get in Ozzy's face. "You don't know anything about anything, so from now on you're gonna keep your mouth shut about the Bruiser or I swear I'll rip out your spleen and make you eat it." The spleen line usually works, because it's one of the more mysterious organs and so any threat involving it is deeply troubling. In this case, however, Ozzy O'Dell has his own deeply troubling response.

"You're a nut job, just like him—even Katrina thinks so! She told me!"

As I reel from this below-the-belt blow, more kids begin to gather. Now my voice comes out as a warning growl. "You have until the count of three to get out of my sight."

He doesn't even wait for the count; he starts swinging

right away—the same odd, roundhouse punches but much more powerful than they were in second grade. I'm caught off guard, and he lands one right on my mouth, then backs away to let it sink in.

Part of me welcomes this chance to put Ozzy in his place—but suddenly I realize something. Brew is holding his mouth. It's bleeding. It's swelling. He's taken the punch Ozzy landed on me! I'm pretty sure I can beat Ozzy in a fight but not without taking substantial damage of my own. *But any damage I take will bounce right to Brew . . . and everyone will see!* Everyone will know, and his life will become the living hell he's feared for so long.

I can't let that happen.

The only way to prevent outing him as an empath is to end this quickly and decisively. I can't just take Ozzy down . . . I have to take him *out*. And fast.

I fend off Ozzy's next round of swings, and he backs off for a moment of taunting.

"You think you're so smart, so cool," Ozzy says, "like the world owes you something because of it."

"I don't want to fight you, Ozzy."

"Yeah, I'll bet you don't!" And he comes at me again.

There's a set of unspoken rules we live by when it comes to fighting. We can't help it. It comes from living in a civilized world. Even when you're fighting your hardest, somewhere deep down, you know how far you can go. But today the rules are gone. Today I fight not to win, but to destroy.

I start in on Ozzy with perfectly controlled methodology.

A sharp sock to the eye: He's slightly dazed.

An upper cut to the chin: His head snaps back.

A powerful piston-punch to the gut: He doubles over, his face jutting toward me.

Then the fourth and final punch. Holding nothing back, I put the full force of my will behind my fist and send it on a decimating collision course with his nose.

I feel bone breaking against my knuckles. He stumbles back, and blood immediately begins to gush from his face, spilling onto the ground. He collapses to his knees, screaming and bringing his hands to his face. He's forgotten the fight; he's forgotten me; all that's left for Ozzy in this moment is the blood, the pain, and the pavement.

The crowd around us that was so quick to cheer and jeer now falls silent behind Ozzy's wet, nasal wails.

Crippendorf looks at me and shakes his head. "Dude, that was so . . . uncalled for."

All I can do is stand there and stare at Ozzy as he bleeds on the sidewalk until Brew grabs me and pulls me away.

48) FALLOUT

"Thanks for taking out the team's star sprinter," Brontë says when Brewster and I get home. Somehow the news got home even before we did. "Do you realize you've just turned Ozzy from a standard school ass into a sympathetic victim? Was that your intent?"

"It was self-defense!" I tell her. "There are witnesses to prove it!"

"Witnesses enough to keep you out of juvie?"

The thought hadn't even occurred to me. "Yes," I tell her, then Brew chimes in.

"Ozzy started it—everyone heard Tennyson say he didn't want to fight, but Ozzy came after him." He gives her the details—how I had stood up for him. She is both horrified and impressed by the smoothie backwash, which I suspect will go down in local history.

"Someday, Tennyson," she says, "I'm convinced there'll be bulletproof glass and armed guards between our conversations."

"Ozzy has lots of friends," says Brew. "What if his friends lie and say you started it?"

"Relax," I tell Brew, impressed by my own calmness.

Even my parents, whose reaction-factor could usually rattle the house off its foundations, are unexpectedly rational. Dad sits me down calmly for the obligatory "What were you thinking?" speech and talks about putting me in an anger management program.

"I wasn't angry when I hit him," I tell him—which is true. I probably should have been, but I wasn't. I was just taking care of a problem.

He and Mom call the O'Dells and offer to pay all of Ozzy's medical expenses; but the O'Dells—who are disgusted both with me and with their own son—refuse, and want to have absolutely nothing to do with us. The threat of a lawsuit looms like a storm cell.

And yet, in spite of all that, things seem as normal as normal can be. Mom and Dad sit in the family room together—in separate chairs, but still in the same room—sharing communal laughter as they watch a dumb sitcom.

I spend most of the night sitting at my desk trying to do homework while fielding calls from my friends—since everyone who wasn't there wants to know how it went down.

When I hang up from one of the calls, I see Cody standing right beside me. I jump a little, not expecting him to be there.

"Is it true you killed a kid?" he asks.

"No!" I tell him. "I broke his nose."

"Oh." Cody seems both relieved and disappointed. "Well, ninjas know how to break your nose so the bone goes right into your brain and you die."

"I'm not a ninja," I remind him. He seems both relieved and disappointed by that, too. Then he thinks about it some more. "Are you gonna get like Uncle Hoyt?" he asks, then he looks at me, waiting for an answer. It makes me shiver, because I know he's looking for something in my eyes—maybe something he saw in his uncle's eyes—and I hope to God he hasn't found it in mine.

"I'll never hit you or your brother, Cody."

"That's not what I mean. . . ." And still he's looking. A little kid's gaze can be innocent; but sometimes their eyes are so wide, they catch all kinds of things older eyes don't. Kind of like those radio telescopes that stare at empty space so hard and so long they find thousands of galaxies in the darkness. Cody's gaze reaches a little too deep, and I have to look away.

"Just don't be like him, okay?" he says, then he leaves, and I'm glad for it—because once he's gone I start to feel pretty good about things. Not just good, but great. In fact, I fall asleep that night feeling a bizarre bliss that flies in the face of everything going on in my life. I know I should probably wonder why, but who questions a good feeling? Better to just enjoy it. The fight with Ozzy seems too small and too far away to matter. So do the old fights between my parents. Ancient history. And all the fallout is little more than stardust settling on my shoulders.

Contentment. I could get used to this feeling.

CODY

49) STUFF

I didn't mean to do it. I just wasn't thinking. Well, that's not true; I *was* thinking, just not the way I needed to be. Uncle Hoyt woulda taught me a lesson if he was here to see it. We were out at the park playing basketball again. That is, Tenny, Brew, and Mr. Sternberger were playing. Me, I don't play because I don't care much for things I'm not already good at, like handball and running, and most other stuff. But Tenny, he gave me a brand-new kite, then he put me with it out in the empty soccer field next to the basketball court and said, "Knock yourself out."

The problem with kites is they got a mind of their own. This one was painted like a hawk, which I guess was right for it, because it sure was a birdbrain the way it kept diving into the ground.

I went over to see if maybe Tenny or Brew or Mr. Sternberger could give me some help, but they were already in a game with a bunch of other people. Brew was playing like one of them. Real good. Maybe not good like me at running, but good enough to score a couple of baskets while I watched.

Uncle Hoyt woulda never let him do that. He'd never let Brew out with a whole bunch of people like that. He'd come out here if he saw it and drag Brew's butt home.

"You weren't meant to be part of things, boy," he'd tell Brew. *"You know it as well as I do."* And Brew would put his head down and follow Uncle Hoyt home, because he'd know Uncle Hoyt was only looking out for him.

But there's no one to protect Brew now, because there he was, playin' up a storm and havin' a good time with a bunch of people who are strangers now but might not be strangers for long. Uncle Hoyt wouldn't be happy; and thinking about Uncle Hoyt makes me sad, because I miss him, or at least I miss the part of him that didn't go foul. I think about how he'd like to see me finally get a kite up in the air, and so it makes me want to do it even more.

I go back to the field with the kite—that dumb old hawk that don't know up from down—and I'm startin' to feel good about it, because the wind, which at first couldn't decide which way to blow, is now blowing straight; and I know if I run into the wind, I might teach that bird to fly.

I start running, letting out some string behind me, and sure enough I get it in the air. It's trying to dip and twirl, but I won't let it dive. The wind's ripping at its wings, but not tearing them, like it did to my old kite. I give the kite more line, and I keep on running, because if I don't, it'll fall down and I'll have to start over. The thing is, the field doesn't go on forever. In a minute I'm at the edge of it—but even though I'm out of grass, I'm not about to stop. So I let out some more line and keep on running right into the street. It's not a big busy street, but there's cars, though, and maybe they're moving a little too fast. But what am I supposed to do? Let the kite fall down after all that work?

So I'm in the street, and one car hits the brakes, and another car swerves around me; but it's okay, because people around here are good drivers, and I'm sure when they see a kid running with a kite in the street they understand the situation, so they're extra careful. I only almost got hit, and almost don't count.

By the time I get across the street, that hawk is real high, and starting to stay up by itself; and since there's nothing in front of me but a big, bushy hillside that probably has snakes and stuff, I turn right and run along the sidewalk.

I didn't see that stupid old electrical tower until it came out of nowhere and grabbed the kite with its ugly gray arms. In a second the kite's just dangling there, whipping back and forth in the wind, all helpless. And that electrical tower, it's looking down on me, and I can almost hear it go "Ha ha," because sometimes I think things that ain't alive know exactly what they're doing.

Well, I'm not about to let it get away with that. It's a brand-new kite! Then I get to thinking how an electrical tower is almost like a tree, except that its branches are metal and more regular. So I put down the kite string and start climbing with my eye on that dangling bird, because Uncle Hoyt always said *"Keep your eye on the prize,"* although I think he should have also said *"Go after the prize,"* too; and maybe that's why prizes never came his way, because all he ever did was look at them. But I'm doing both, keeping my eye on it and going after it at the same time.

I climb and climb, and for the longest time the kite doesn't seem to get any closer. Finally I get just as high as the kite; but it's still out of reach, dangling on one of those stubby skeleton arms of the tower. Its tail's all wrapped around one of the electric wires that looks much thicker up here than it did from the ground, and the wires are all buzzing like crazy—not just buzzing, but humming, like they all got a voice and are trying to be an electric choir.

I know enough not to touch those wires since I might get electrocuted—but I also know that birds sometimes sit on electric wires and are fine, so maybe it's not as dangerous as they say. Either way, though, I have to get my kite down, so I work my way toward it. In a minute I'm out on the arm, and I can feel all the electricity making my arm hairs stand on end even in the wind. The kite's still just out of reach, dangling and twisting and teasing me, so I reach for it with one hand.

Then I look down.

Maybe if I had looked down sooner I would have chickened out and gone back down, because there's no tree I've ever climbed that's this high. It's like I've suddenly forgotten how to climb, because there I am, clinging to the metal bar with both my arms and both my legs and my whole body as well, and now I notice for the first time how cold the wind is, and the kite, which just a second ago looked like it was teasing me, now just looks trapped and kind of sad.

From way up there I can see everything. The field seems bigger than it did from the ground, but the basketball court looks smaller. No one's on the court anymore. Instead they're all running toward me across the soccer field. Even the people I don't know. I hear a whole lot of "There he is!" and "Oh, my God!" and "Hold on!"

Brew gets to the tower first, with Tenny right behind. They talk for a split second, and Tenny runs off, I guess to get help, although I can't see why since a whole lot of help is running toward the tower already. Then Brew starts to climb. He was never much of a climber, but I guess he is when it's important, because he climbs the tower pretty good. Down below there's like a million people looking up at me, their eyes on the prize.

Halfway up the tower, Brew slips and catches himself, banging against a bar, and the metal rings out like a bell.

"Go that way!" I yell, pointing to a place where the metal's all rusted and rough, because that's easier for sneakers to grip onto.

The closer he gets, the less scared I am, because I know that my brother's going to save me. When he's almost as high as me, I tell him I'm sorry for getting stuck up here.

"Stay absolutely still!" he tells me. Then he comes a little closer. Down beneath us, Tennyson runs back with what looks like a bundle of flowers; but when he gets to Mr. Sternberger, he takes a part of it and the bundle gets bigger. Mr. Sternberger starts giving orders to the people around him, and they grab on to it, too. That's when I realize that it's not flowers at all—it's a flowery sheet, and Mr. Sternberger's getting everyone to stretch it out beneath us until it's pulled tight, like a trampoline made of roses and daisies. It takes maybe ten people to stretch it out, but from up in the tower it still looks small.

Finally Brew's right next to me, but I'm still just out of reach to him. He's scared—*real* scared, but I'm not anymore, because he won't let me be. Brew never lets me be scared.

"I'm almost there! Don't move!"

"How'm I gonna get offa here if I don't move?"

Then, holding tight to the tower, he looks at me in that deep kind of way, like teachers before they send you to the principal.

"You have to stop doing these things," he says.

"The kite got stuck; I had to get it down. I was just being responsible."

"Be responsible on the ground!"

He tries to get closer but can't. Still, he's not giving up. "You're gonna be okay," he tells me.

"I know I am." And it's true. I know it for sure, because Brew's there.

I hear sirens getting closer, and before long a police car comes in from one direction and a fire truck from another. I start looking around because if there's a fire, I'm sure to see it from up here. Then they both stop right in front of the electrical tower and I get it. Fire trucks don't always come because of fires. Sometimes they come to get cats out of trees. Or people out of towers.

Maybe it's because I'm thinking about the fire truck, or maybe it's because my fingers have gotten so cold, but I start to slip.

"No!" yells Brew. I grab onto the bar and my legs slip off, but I get them wrapped around again, losing a sneaker that somehow got untied along the way. It tumbles down and down, totally missing the flowery sheet. Instead it hits some lady in the head, and I hear her go "Ooof!" I want to laugh, but I don't, because laughing might make me slip again.

The fire truck is the kind with a big ladder; but it takes time to get it working, and I don't have a whole lot of time, because there's no more grip left in my fingers at all. I know if I fall I'll hit that lady in the head, too. Brew will take the fall away from me even before I feel it, so it won't hurt me; but it would *definitely* hurt Brew. Then he'd be all mad at me like he was the time I broke his arm.

I slip again, and this time I know there's no stopping it, so rather than falling straight, I stretch out both my hands toward Brew.

"Cody!"

He catches me by one wrist, and we hold on to each other. I swing and twist from his arm like the kite swinging and twisting on its string.

Brew holds on to me with all his strength.

"Don't worry," I tell him. "I'll be okay."

"But I won't!" he says through his teeth.

"You'll get better," I remind him.

But he doesn't answer me.

"You always get better. . . ."

He still doesn't say anything, because every last bit of him is holding on to me, even his voice.

That's the first time I realize that maybe there are things he won't get better from. What if there are some things that will make him dead like Uncle Hoyt, and he'll get burned down to dust, and put in a cardboard box, too? The thought of it scares me. It scares me more than being up in the tower, more than falling, more than anything.

I can feel all that *scaredness* trying to sneak out of me and into Brew, but I won't let it. I hold on to my scared, because I know it's making my hand stronger. Without that scaredness

I'll fall. It's the only thing giving my fingers strength enough to hold on to his.

And I know I've just done the impossible, because holding on to *anything* bad when I'm with Brew has always been impossible—not just the ouches, but the bad feelings, too. But maybe it's not impossible. . . . Maybe I just have to *want* to hold it . . . because as I hang here, I'm scared as anything, and I stay that way because I want to.

The fear in my fingers makes them squeeze tighter until my knuckles turn white. Until it feels like my hand'll fall off. Until I hear a voice behind me say "I've got you!" and an arm grabs me from behind, pulling me onto the ladder that has finally gotten up to us.

"You're safe, son," the firefighter says.

Even before he takes me down that ladder, I know I'll be okay, and Brew will be okay, too. Because Brew can do his big impossible; but today, by holding on to my scaredness, I did my own little impossible, too.

50) PRECIPICE

I can't deny that things were changing in our family. It began at the very moment Brewster and Cody moved in; but it grew slowly, subtly enough for me to believe it was my own simple optimism. You see, when things are finally starting to go right after a whole lot of wrong, you can either focus on the good, or you can zero in on everything else that isn't.

Most people go one way or the other: the glass half full or the glass half empty. It's a rare skill to be able to see it both ways at the same time, and I, unfortunately, do not have that skill. All I could see was that Brew and his brother were saved, and my derailed family was back on sturdy tracks, thank you very much.

Yet as right as things were, Brew was having a harder and harder time. It was worse when he was home. He was constantly exhausted, like the walls themselves were draining life away from him. He was constantly on edge, like our house was teetering on a precipice that only he could see.

And then he saved Cody from the tower.

I wasn't there when it happened, but half a dozen people captured it on video. It made the news, and turned Brew into an overnight hero—and although his fame lasted for the typical fifteen minutes, the shadow under which he had always lived was obliterated by the spotlight. That should have been a good thing.

51) BANDWAGON

"Hi, Brontë, mind if we sit by you?"

It was Amanda Milner and Joe Crippendorf, who may or may not have been an item—and enjoyed maintaining the mystery. This was the third visitation at our lunch table that day by unexpected apparitions.

"We were just leaving," Brew said.

I put my hand over his, which was sufficient enough to keep him from bolting. "No we weren't." I slowly began eating some questionable Jell-O that I had originally planned to avoid. "Have a seat."

They slid in with us. Amanda is what I would call a mid-range friend. Not close enough to share deep secrets with but certainly close enough to choose each other as partners for the occasional class project. Joe is the easygoing kind of goofball you don't mind having around, unless he's surrounded by other such goofballs.

"We think what you did was great, Brewster!" Amanda said.

Everyone knew about it—if they hadn't caught the news, they had heard it on morning announcements, when the principal lauded Brew's feat and awarded him an honorary varsity letter.

"It was no big deal," Brew said modestly, clearly wishing this would all go away.

Joe rapped him on the arm. "Man, I don't know if I would've had the guts to do that. Way up there? All that electricity?"

Brew just shrugged. "I had to—he's my brother."

"Yeah," said Joe. "I've got a brother, too. And if he was up there and it was up to me to save him, his name would probably be *Splat* right now."

They asked us about how it happened, then talked a bit about the whole foster thing and how cool our parents are to let Brew and me live under the same roof.

"We have a strict rule that we're just friends at home," I told them. "We're only dating when we're out of the house." And since we were currently out of the house, I rubbed his arm, taking advantage of the fact.

"I'd break that rule in five minutes," said Joe. Amanda nudged him with her elbow, and he laughed. Brew laughed a little, too, before he caught himself.

"So listen," said Amanda, pulling out two envelopes with heart stickers sealing them closed. "I know it's corny and all, but my parents are throwing me a sweet sixteen, and I wanted to invite you two." She handed Brew an invitation, and he just stared at it. "I hope you can make it."

"I'm sure we can," I said before Brew could respond. "Thank you."

Amanda got up and left, satisfied, but Joe lingered. "Hey, Brewster," he said, "all the years I've known you, I've kinda been an idiot. Maybe not as bad as Ozzy, but still, I was."

"Don't worry about it," Brew said.

But Joe wouldn't let it go as fast as that. I found that admirable. "Well, it wasn't right. I'm sorry. I just want you to know that I, for one, think you're okay."

"Thanks, Crippendorf." And the fact that Brew called him by his last name solidified their friendship. Joe left, and Brew just sat there kind of dazzled—and with good reason. This was more than just my handpicked circle of close friends; this was a grassroots movement. People love jumping on bandwagons, and no bandwagon is more inviting than that of an unassuming hero. Sure, Brew might just have been the flavor of the week and next week everyone would forget, but some of these newfound friendships were bound to linger. I gave him a hug tight enough to adjust his spine in a chiropractic sort of way.

"See?" I told him. "Everything's changing for you."

He tucked his invitation into his pocket and didn't say a word.

52) CLANDESTINE

That night, after everyone else had gone to bed, I went downstairs for a midnight snack. I couldn't help but peek in through the open door of the guest room as I passed, admittedly hoping to catch a fleeting glimpse of Brew in his boxers, which I have only seen when it's my turn to fold the laundry.

Brew was sitting up in bed, fully dressed, knees to chest; and his forehead was beaded with sweat.

"Brew?"

He rolled out his shoulders. "Cody had a nightmare," he said, although from what I could see, Cody was sleeping soundly. Brew, on the other hand, showed no sign of having slept at all.

I sat down on the edge of the bed. "If something's wrong and you want to talk about it . . ."

He didn't say anything at first. Then he lowered his head,

shaking it. "I just . . . I just don't think I can *do* this, Brontë."

"No one's expecting you to do anything."

But when he turned to me, the weighty look in his eyes said otherwise. I glanced away.

"I've been thinking about Uncle Hoyt," he said.

The mention of the man's name made me uncomfortable. I know we should have respect for the dead, but why should we respect those who hadn't earned it in life?

"Uncle Hoyt told me to hate the world—that it was the only way I'd survive."

"What a terrible thing to say."

"But what if he was right?" He looked at me, pleading for me to tell him that his uncle was wrong. I wanted to hold him, but that would be breaking the golden rule. While in this house, Brew could not be my boyfriend. An awful rule . . . but considering the fact that I was sitting on his bed in a clandestine midnight encounter, feeling the things I was feeling, well . . . that made it a necessary awful rule.

"Your uncle was *not* right. About anything," I told him. "What's the point of living if you're going to hate the world? Guard your heart if you have to, but don't shut it away."

He smiled. "'*Guard your heart.*' My mother used to say that." It was the first time he'd ever spoken of his mother. I waited for more, but that's all he chose to share.

"It's going to be fine," I told him. "I'll see you in the morning."

I got up to leave, but before I reached the threshold, he said:

"I killed my uncle."

I froze in the doorway. There were a hundred different things that flew through my mind at that moment. Everything from Most Likely to Receive the Death Penalty to the unthinkable concept that all those ridiculous school rumors could be right. But I had enough rational thoughts swimming around to see through to what he meant rather than what he had said. I turned back to him.

"Your uncle died of a stroke."

"Yes," Brew admitted. "But I was there. I could have saved him. He asked me to, but instead I left him to die."

Hearing that left me speechless for a moment. I took a look at his left leg—the one that had developed the sudden, strange limp. That wasn't a twisted ankle; it wasn't going away. Only now did I realize where it had come from, and why he harbored such guilt. The thought of Uncle Hoyt putting Brew in that position—of asking Brew to die for him—just made me even more furious at that miserable man.

"You took more than your share of pain from him," I pointed out. "That day, and every day before. It was *his* life to lose, not yours."

He nodded; but it was just an acknowledgment, not acceptance. I don't know if anything anyone could say would convince him. It's hard to understand how someone who has such power to transform the lives of those he touches could still feel so desperate for redemption.

"Your uncle *used* you, right down to the moment he died," I told him. "I swear to you, Brew, no one's ever going to use you like that again."

TENNYSON

53) EJECTION

I'm off my game, and I'm not feeling right.

The coach knows that something's up with me. He pulls me out at the half. We're down 6 to 3 against an easy team. I haven't scored once.

I'm nervous and unsettled. I tell myself it's because Katrina's not at the game. She's always at the game. She's kind of like my good-luck charm. I keep hoping she'll show up and that when she does I'll be able to get my head clear. What's more, my lack of focus is contagious. I guess I affect the mood of the team far more than I realize, because my teammates keep missing passes and obvious opportunities to score, getting crankier by the minute.

It's Katrina. Has to be. She didn't even text to let me know she wasn't coming. She hasn't called or texted me for two days; and when I call her, I just get left in voice mail purgatory.

I watch the game, miserable on the bench as we give up another goal. By the fourth quarter all I want to do is go home.

We're shut out by one of the worst teams in the league. While the other team celebrates their surreal and unexpected victory, our coach lays into us, which is just what we deserve—or at least I deserve it. If we lose one more game, we won't even qualify for league finals. Killer practices all next week.

I should go straight home, but I don't. Instead I take a detour to Ahab's—our neighborhood coffeehouse trying painfully hard to be Starbucks, down to the obvious rip-off names of their drinks. I figure I'll stop in for a Phrappuccino to console myself, but even before I reach for the door, I see them inside.

Katrina sits beside a bald kid with a bandaged face.

And his hand is on her knee.

All of a sudden it's Mom and the fur ball all over again; and I keep walking, never going inside, trying to figure out which of the two sights is worse: Mom and her boyfriend or Katrina and Ozzy. Now more than ever I just want to get home.

So Katrina's playing nurse again, just like she did when we first started going out. She's taken in the wounded while hitting my ejection button in one smooth stroke. And how unfair is it that I can't even walk in there and punch him out since I already broke his freaking nose?

Home! The second I get in the front door and close it behind me, I start to feel better. I find Brontë in the living room working on some project with Brewster. Papers are spread on the coffee table.

Brontë looks up when she sees me. "How was the game?" she asks.

"They lost," Brew says.

"How can you tell?" she asks.

"Isn't it obvious?"

"The game went fine," I say, not wanting to get into it. It's over. Now that I'm home, it's history. Even thinking about Ozzy and Katrina doesn't feel quite so horrifying.

In the kitchen, Mom marinates meat for Dad, who's out back getting the barbecue going—something he rarely does this time of year. I scavenge the fridge, and Mom says, "Don't ruin your appetite!"

Normal.

How could anything be wrong when everything at home feels so perfectly normal?

By the time I get up to my room and stretch out on my bed, I can feel the last of my frustration leave me. It feels like I'm enveloped in an invisible security blanket. All is well with the world. And all will be well with Katrina—because I'm already working the angles, formulating a plan. There are two things that go straight to Katrina's heart: injury and victory. Well, Ozzy's got injury all locked up—but victory is mine. Or at least it will be.

54) AGENDUM

I wouldn't say I'm a selfish person. No more than anyone else. When it comes down to it, everyone has an agenda, even if we don't know what it is at the time. There are lots of times I'll do the right thing even if it's against my own self-interest, too. It all depends on the circumstances. There are things that shift the balance, though. I know exactly where that balance has shifted when I go into Brewster and Cody's room that night.

Cody lies on the blow-up mattress, lost in a comic book, while Brew reads a skinny little book of poetry that most guys wouldn't be caught dead with. His eyes rise over the edge of the book and meet mine.

"You were right about us losing the game," I tell him.

He turns a page in his book. "It doesn't take a brain surgeon."

"No, I guess not." I fiddle with the doorknob for a moment. "Well, I just wanted to let you know that I've changed my mind."

"About what?"

"About you coming to my games."

Now he puts down the book, getting more interested. "Why?"

I shrug like it's nothing. "Just because."

"Maybe I don't want to be at your games."

"Suit yourself." I turn to leave.

He stops me. I knew he'd stop me. "Maybe I'll come if you tell me the truth."

And so I do. Or at least part of it. "Our team needs to win the next few games to qualify for league finals," I tell him. I don't talk about Katrina since he doesn't like her anyway. "If I play well enough, I might even be in the running for MVP."

That's when Cody looks up from his comic book, and I realize that he wasn't in his own superhero universe at all—he's been right here all along, listening to everything. He knows what I'm asking Brew to do. He knows what it means. Suddenly I feel guilty, like maybe I don't want a witness.

Brew picks up his book again and pretends to read, but his concentration isn't there like it was before. "I thought you said it was cheating."

"I said it *feels* like cheating. There's a difference."

"I'll think about it," he says, but I know he's already decided to do it. It would all be good if it weren't for Cody. Those eyes of his just look up at me, pupils dilated in the diffused light of the room. Wide, black pools, seeking out galaxies.

55) UNPRECEDENTED

Brew and I have an understanding. Brew and I are a team on the field. So what if the coach doesn't know he has a secret player? I start the game feeling like I can take on the world, but today we're just taking on the Billington Bullets. They're highly ranked, and a tough team to beat—but I make it clear what kind of game this is going to be right away. I score in the first minute of play. From the first face-off, I rule the field with unprecedented speed and agility—rising from hard falls, disregarding the hardest of stick checks, and never losing an ounce of energy. I'm golden.

And Katrina is there to see it. I made her promise to come.

"I need you there," I had told her. "Please . . . you inspire me."

I hated to beg, but she has to see me. It will all be for nothing if she doesn't see.

I keep glancing over at Brew, just to check in and see how he's holding up. He paces off by himself at the edge of the field, a little worn, a little out of breath. He leans back against the fence and gives me a thumbs-up. I resolve that if I get MVP, I'll give him the trophy. I'll keep Katrina.

Halftime! It's 4 to 1—and I scored all four goals. The coach smiles and looks at me like I'm his own son. "That's what I'm talking about, Tennyson!" he says. "Show 'em what we're made of!"

"Can I stay in for the whole game?"

"Keep playing like that and you can stay in till New Year's!"

The rest of the game is a study in humiliation for the Bullets. With thirty seconds remaining, I seal the Bullets' fate by scoring my sixth goal of the game. I've scored six of our eight goals.

The whistle blows, and it's all over! My team races to me, and in a second I'm lifted up in the air—levitation by glory! But I don't bask for too long. As soon as I'm back down on the ground, I'm bounding over to Katrina.

"I'm glad you came!" I pull her in for a quick kiss. She doesn't resist, but she does try to pull away after a second, because, after all, I'm sweaty.

"Sorry," I tell her. "I'll shower and we'll go out to celebrate."

"You should celebrate with the team."

"Plenty of time for that!"

"Listen, Tennyson . . . I'm happy for you and all, and you were great out there, you really were . . . but I'm meeting Ozzy."

I'm listening, but I'm not really hearing, because I'm not over myself yet. "So ditch him," I tell her. "I know you feel sorry for him and all, and I know I shouldn't have hit him so hard, and you're right about how all the stuff going on between my parents was driving me crazy—but I'm okay now." I put my arm around her, and she pulls away again.

"It's not about feeling sorry for him. . . . I was seeing him even before you broke his nose."

Suddenly it's like I've been smashed in the head with my own lacrosse stick. My million-dollar words get knocked out of my skull, and all I can say is:

"Huh?"

"Actually," she says, "I kind of thought that might be why you were fighting him."

"Whuh?"

"I was a little flattered, to tell you the truth." Then she leans forward and kisses me, but on the forehead, the way you might kiss a small child, or an old dog before putting it to sleep. "You should call Katy Barnett—I know for a fact she's been dying to go out with you since, like, the Plasticine era."

"Pleistocene," I mumble vacantly.

"Right, that one. Well, toodles!"

And she's gone, strolling away with all the good feelings I thought were mine.

The crash inside me could shake the earth. It feels like a fever. It feels like the flu. And my team is still celebrating. We've won the game, and qualified for league finals. Why do I not care?

There's no rock large enough for me to crawl under right now, and all I want to do is get home—teleport if I could—straight to my bedroom.

In all the commotion I've totally forgotten about Brew. I look for him, but he's gone. He must have left the second the game was over—gone home to nurse my wounds, whatever they might be. Did I get hurt in this game? A little banged up maybe, but nothing major—nothing he didn't sign on for. I want to find him and talk to him. I need to have someone to commiserate with. Even if he doesn't talk back, that's okay.

I say my good-byes to the team as fast as I can, grab my lacrosse stick, and head home, feeling like I might use my stick to take out a few mailboxes along the way, and wonder how I got so psychotic.

56) PACIFIED

Brontë catches me out in the street before I get to the front door and punches me in the arm with the strength of a prize-fighter.

"Ow!"

"That's for forcing him to go to your game!"

I guess Brew got home before me. I guess he told her. Or more likely she saw the way he looked, and she dragged it out of him.

"I didn't force him to do anything. He came because he wanted to."

But she's not buying a word of it. "You're a self-centered, self-serving—"

"Oh, and when I chased him away from my game last time, that was wrong, too?"

She fumbles her thoughts a bit. "Yes, it was—but at least

then you were thinking of him, not yourself!"

I don't want to fight with her; I just want to get inside. The things I'm feeling right now are too venomous to put into words, and I don't want to take it out on her or on anyone—I just want to get past her and in through the door.

"Instead of complaining about me," I tell her, "maybe you should think about what *you* just did to him!" She looks at me, not understanding. So I rub the fresh charley horse in my arm from her punch and say: "The second I walk inside, he's gonna have one nasty bruise thanks to you."

I push past her and go into the house, leaving her to stew in her own juices.

Once inside, I drop my lacrosse stick on the family room floor and collapse onto the sofa. I curl up and close my eyes like I do when I have a bad stomachache. I feel my diaphragm begin to heave, and it makes me furious that I might actually burst into tears. Me. I don't *do* that! No one can ever see me do that. Is it wrong to feel this awful when you get dumped? Is this even about Katrina at all? I don't know. I don't care. I just want the feeling gone.

I hear the TV turn on, and I open my eyes to see that Cody has entered the room. He looks at the way I'm all curled up on the sofa and says, "Can I watch cartoons?"

"Do whatever you want," I tell him.

He sits on the floor in front of me but leaves the volume a little too low to hear. "Are you just tired, or do you got bad stuff?" he asks me.

"Don't worry about it," I tell him. "It's not your problem."

"If you got bad stuff, you should leave," he says.

"What are you talking about? I just got home."

"You should leave anyway." Then he presses the remote, and the volume gets higher and higher until it's blasting.

I take the remote away from him and turn off the TV. "What's your problem?"

Then he turns on me with a vengeance. "It ain't fair! He's MY brother, and you got no right!"

I want to yell back at him, sink down to his level; but then something begins to change. I feel it building like a wave gathering strength just before it crashes on the shore.

Relief. I draw a deep, fulfilling breath. *Comfort.* I slowly let it out. *Contentment.* I am pacified, just as I've been pacified each day when I get home. It usually doesn't arrive so powerfully, but then, I'm usually not feeling as beaten down as I am today. As I *was* today.

All the bad emotions I had just a few moments ago are gone. I'm a bit dizzy and almost weightless. It feels good.

Cody's shoulders slump, and he sits back down. "Too late."

Now I can't deny that this is something more than the mere comfort of being in a place that's safe and familiar. "Cody . . . what just happened?"

"The bad stuff went away," he said like it was perfectly

obvious, perfectly natural. "Cuts and stuff are easy—they go quicker; but the stuff inside is harder. It's like it has to find a way out first."

I hear muffled sobs from the guest room, on the other side of the wall. The sobs are coming from Brew. They're deep; they're powerful; they're mine. But not anymore.

"He can take it," Cody says, resigned. "He can take anything."

By the time I get to the guest room, Brontë's already there, holding Brew, trying to wrap her slender arms around his hulking frame as he shudders with sobs of both fury and sorrow. There's a welt on his arm where Brontë punched me.

"What is it, Brew, what's wrong?" Brontë says, at a loss to comfort him. "Tell me, please; I want to help!"

The second he sees me, he looks up at me with pleading eyes—he knows this came from me. He knows! "What happened, Tennyson? You won the game; what happened?"

I can only stutter there in the doorway.

Brontë narrows her eyes at me. "Get out!" But I don't move, so she gets up and reaches for the door. "I said, get out!" Then she slams the door in my face. I wonder if she even knows what's going on. I wonder if he'll tell her. Brontë, the compassionate, Brontë, the observant. I'll bet she's totally in the dark when it comes to this secret side of Brewster's gift.

But now I know—and knowing the full truth propels me out the front door. I can't be a part of this. I can't willingly bury him in all my baggage.

I make it as far as the front gate before my momentum fails me. There, just a few feet away from the street, I can feel the edge of Brewster's influence. I can feel myself slipping out of range. All the bad feelings—the hurt, the betrayal—it's all waiting there just on the other side of that gate. One more step and it will all come flooding back. And as much as I want to take that step, as much as I want to free Brew from the pain . . . I can't. I've always considered myself so strong, so willful; but here is the truth: I don't even have the strength of will to steal back my own misery.

Dejected, defeated, I go back inside; but in a few moments even that crushing sense of defeat is gone, evaporating into nothing as I sit in the family room with Cody, the two of us watching cartoons without a care in the world.

BRONTË

57) ABJECT

Tennyson began to act strange around the time he and Katrina broke up, and his behavior became odder and odder each day. It came to a peak the day Brew and I went to Amanda Milner's sweet sixteen. When we got home that night, he laid into us the second we walked in the door.

"Where were you? What were you doing? Do you know what time it is?"

He sounded like a parent on the rampage, and his eyes were disturbingly wild. Tennyson had always been unnecessarily protective of me, but this was ridiculous. Brew was getting all stressed out and went straight to the bathroom, just to get out of Tennyson's line of fire.

"What is wrong with you!" I demanded once Brew was gone.

"You shouldn't be taking him out like this!"

"What is he—a dog on a leash?"

"No, it's just that . . . it's just that you need to be careful."

I pointed an accusing finger at him. "You're telling me to be careful? You, who treated yourself to a pain-free lacrosse victory at his expense?"

Just mentioning it deflated him. He looked at me pleadingly—a helpless look that, until recently, was never in my brother's arsenal of facial expressions. Lately, there'd been a whole lot of weird desperation in his eyes, and in his actions. If I didn't know better, I'd wonder if Tennyson was on drugs.

"Mom and Dad were fighting while you were gone."

It surprised me, because they hadn't had an argument for a while. "Fighting how?"

"Like they used to." He looked at me for a moment more with that abject expression, but then his face changed. It was as if every muscle in his face switched to a new preset. He took a deep breath and relaxed, his anxiety fading like a dark cloud dissipating. I'd noticed that before, too—how he'd be so anxious and then calm down so quickly. He took another deep breath and released it.

"It's okay now," he said. "It's okay—but you shouldn't keep Brew out so long. He's not used to parties and all those people."

"Now you sound like his uncle," I told him. I just meant it as a tiny little poison-tipped barb, but somehow it hit deep. He couldn't even answer me. He just turned and retreated to his room.

I could have gone after him and worked on him, ferreting out exactly what was going on, but I was too disgusted with Tennyson to pursue it. Instead I checked in on Mom and Dad. If they had been fighting, then there was some fresh hell we'd all have to deal with.

I found them both sitting up in bed, just inches away from each other, calmly reading.

"Was it a nice party, honey?" Mom asked once she saw me standing there. I saw no evidence of emotional battle scars on either of them: They hadn't retreated to neutral corners of the house; neither one was pacing, or brooding, or scarfing down comfort food.

"It was fine," I said; and without the patience to beat around the bush, I asked, "What were you guys arguing about?"

They looked at each other a bit perplexed by the question. For a moment I thought Tennyson must have been lying until Dad said, "Well, whatever it was, it must not have been too important."

Mom concurred, and they both returned to their books.

I told them good night and retreated to my own room, feeling content with their answers, with the evening, with myself. I didn't even harbor any ill feelings toward my brother, which was a definite indication that something was off—not just *around* me but *inside* me as well. Still, I chose to ignore it, subconsciously citing all those wonderful sayings that justify denial:

What you don't know can't hurt you.
Let sleeping dogs lie.
Don't look a gift horse in the mouth.

I keep telling myself that if I had questioned things sooner—if I had grasped the extent to which Brew had become intertwined in our lives—I would have behaved differently. I would have done the right thing. But who am I kidding? How can you do the right thing when you can't figure out what that thing is? When all you have before you are choices in various shades of wrong?

58) INTERLOPER

Tennyson and I always made fun of people who blindly followed the crowd. Lemmings, we called them—poor, unfortunate creatures who, at the slightest sign of rain, relinquish their self-determination to the mob and join a mad, mindless stampede. Ultimately the stampede leads them off a cliff into the sea, where they all drown. It's funny if you're an observer. It's tragic if you're a lemming.

I understand lemmings now. I understand that, contrary to popular opinion, it takes only two to form a crowd. Perhaps a brother and a sister. I can't say I was blindly following Tennyson, but I was so busy noticing what was wrong with *him* that I failed to see that I was charging toward the same cliff right beside him.

We had an unexpected guest the following evening.

I had the misfortune of being the one to answer the door. Standing there was a small man with lots of hair and a thick but well-groomed beard. I recognized him from various university functions as one of our parents' colleagues.

"I'd like to speak with your mother," he said with a slight accent that I couldn't place. He was determined yet fidgety, his eyes intense and a little wild. All at once I realized who this was. This was the man Mom was seeing. Mr. Monday Night.

I felt a wave of panic rise in me, brimming into anger; but the feeling drained quickly. This was my house, I was in control of the doorway, and this interloper was not getting in.

"You'd better get out of here," I told him, coldly staring him down, "before my father sees you."

And then from behind me, I heard, "I already have."

My father was standing halfway down the stairs, gripping the railing. He stood there for a long moment, and I saw the same rise and fall of anger that I had felt—although I'm sure his blossomed even more powerfully before it subsided. He came the rest of the way down the stairs, and when he spoke he was like a diplomat, with both power and poise in his voice; but his anger was reined in.

"Well, if it isn't the proverbial barbarian at the gate," Dad said. "Are you coming in, Bob, or are you going to stand in the doorway all night?"

The man stepped in; and Dad approached him, looked

him over, and grunted dismissively. "This is Dr. Thorlock, from the anthropology department. An expert in prehistoric man, and other small-minded things."

I heard a guffaw behind me and turned to see Tennyson peering down from the top of the stairs; but the moment I saw him, he retreated.

"Are you here to bring us a little drama today, Bob?" Dad asked. "Are you going to challenge me to a duel?"

Thorlock seemed entirely unnerved by Dad's flipness.

"I just want to talk to Lisa."

"Brontë," said Dad, "please go fetch your mother."

I found Mom in the laundry room, and when I told her that Thorlock was here, she looked shocked; but that faded, too. "Well," she said with a sigh far too light for the circumstance, "we knew it would come to this. No sense postponing the inevitable."

"Which inevitable?" I dared to ask.

But all Mom said was "We'll see."

Then she strode down into the foyer.

I should have been dizzy with dread but instead was merely filled with car-wreck curiosity. At the time I assumed it was a protective layer of numbness. A shock-shell rather than shell shock. I would have eavesdropped on the three of them if I hadn't suddenly heard a groan from the guest room. I went in to find Brew holding his gut, rocking back and forth as he sat on the bed. He was here alone tonight. Cody, who now had actually accumulated a friend or two, was at a sleepover.

"Are you okay?" I asked Brew.

"No," he snapped. "I mean, yes. Just leave me alone, okay?"

He doubled over, moaning in pain through gritted teeth.

"Is it your stomach?" I asked.

"Yes, that's it," he blurted. "Stomach. It's my stomach."

I felt his forehead. He didn't have a fever, but he was clammy. I touched his arm—the skin on his forearm had such goose-flesh, I felt like I was reading Braille. "I'll get you something," I told him, trying to remember what biological nightmare the school gave us for lunch that day. On the way to the medicine chest, I made a point of looking toward the foyer, where Mom spoke to Thorlock in hushed tones. Dad was now sitting on the stairs, observing. He looked somewhat relaxed as he sat there, and I remember thinking how *off* that was; but this particular kind of family drama was not anything I'd experienced before, so how was I to judge what behavior was appropriate when your mother's boyfriend paid a visit? Rather than dwelling on it, I brought Brew some Maalox, which he guzzled straight from the bottle.

"Thank you," he said with the same guttural voice. "I'm better now. You can go."

Then he rolled to face the wall, pulling the covers over his head, ending any hope of conversation.

By the time I left the guest room, Thorlock was gone, and my parents were in the kitchen. Dad was scouring the fridge for some low-carb snack, and Mom was thumbing through a cookbook. I felt like I had suddenly time-warped into a different day.

"So . . . what happened?"

Neither of them answered right away; but when they saw I wasn't leaving until someone said something, Dad chimed in with "Mom asked him to leave, and so he did."

"That's it?" I asked. "He's gone for good?"

"We've set boundaries," Mom said. "Boundaries and rules."

"As in 'Come here again and I'll get a restraining order'?"

Dad laughed at that, and Mom tossed him a halfhearted scowl. "No," said Mom. "Not exactly." Mom turned a page in her cookbook, and I closed the book, practically catching her finger.

"What, then?"

She sighed—again that small kind of sigh that spoke of minor concerns. "Mondays are still Mondays," she said. "My night out."

Usually I'm a quick study, but it took a while for the words to relay from my ears to my brain before settling in my solar plexus like a rock. And in the other room, I could hear Brew groaning again. I turned to Dad, who had a slice of Muenster cheese hanging from his mouth.

"And you're . . . okay with this?"

Dad's eye twitched slightly. "No," he admitted. "But I'll live with it." And then he added, "Maybe I'll take Tuesday nights off."

I snapped my eyes to Mom, certain she would say something like "Over my dead body!" but instead she opened the cookbook again. "Do you think it's too late to start a roast?"

This was wrong.

The things they said, the things they *felt* were wrong to the core—but it wasn't just them. The depth of what I *should* be feeling was absent from me as well. My emotions had become as shallow as a wading pool. I couldn't feel anything but a pleasant, airy void, as incongruous as sunshine in a thunderstorm.

I left my parents in their surreal stupor and took a moment to peer in on Brew. Stomachaches I could understand. They had easy solutions that came in bottles and tasted like chalk. Brew wasn't moaning anymore, but he was breathing heavily and haltingly beneath the covers.

"Can I do something for you?" I asked, feeling helpless but wanting desperately to somehow ease his pain.

"No," he said weakly. "My head's better now. Thank you."

"You said it was your stomach."

"Did I?"

And then I finally connected several of the many dots littering my head. Brew had acted this way after that lacrosse game—the one where Katrina broke up with Tennyson. I had the sudden sneaking suspicion that Tennyson knew something I didn't.

59) INCONGRUOUS

I pushed my way into Tennyson's room without knocking. He was sitting on his bed, a plate of veggies beside him, a textbook in his lap, and his TV playing a bad slasher film.

"Yes?"

He didn't look surprised that I had burst into his room uninvited; he merely waited for me to say something, like he was expecting me to burst in all along.

"Mom and Dad are acting weird, and something's bothering Brew."

"What else is new?" he said. He picked up a carrot and started munching on it. "Is the fur ball gone?"

"Yes, and no," I told him. "But Thorlock's beside the point. You know something, don't you?"

"I know lots of things—your inquiry needs to be more specific."

"Just answer the question."

"True/false, or multiple choice?" he asked.

"How about an essay worth ninety percent of your grade."

He tapped his pen on his textbook. I waited. On screen a woman with bulbous, inorganic breasts was chased by a dwarf wielding an oversize carving knife. I reached over and turned off the TV.

"Feeling ticked off?" Tennyson asked. "Feeling angry?"

"No, not really," I told him honestly.

"Funny," he said. "Neither am I."

"Can you please stop being enigmatic!"

"Yes, and no."

I closed my eyes and sighed. Round and round we always went, my brother and I, always trying to see who was more clever. I folded my arms, content to be silent until Tennyson said something useful.

"I can't tell you what I *don't* know," he said. "I can't comment on what I don't understand."

"So tell me something you *do* understand."

He thought about it and finally said, "I think I might understand his uncle. I know why he wouldn't let Brew have friends. And why he did his best to keep Brew housebound."

"Because he was a sick, sick man!" I reminded my brother.

"Yes," Tennyson agreed. "Sick, and twisted, and cruel. But keeping Brew lonely might have been the one act of kindness he ever did in his entire, miserable life." Then Tennyson turned on the TV to a bloodcurdling scream from the silicon starlet. "Now if you'll excuse me, a sizable body count awaits."

I wanted to be furious at Tennyson's bewildering insensitivity, but I couldn't be. I wanted to be neck-deep in frustration over our parents' psychotically serene behavior, but I couldn't feel that either. The flood of distress I so desperately wanted to hold on to was mercury in my hands: heavy, dense, yet impossible to hold. So I grabbed Tennyson's plate from him and hurled it across the room—anything to shatter the numbness.

The plate didn't even break. It hit the wall and fell onto the bed, dumping carrots, celery, and ranch dressing all over the bedspread.

Tennyson, who should have jumped up and yelled at me, just looked at it and said, "Now look what you've done."

"*Push me!*" I screamed at him. "*Call me an idiot! Tell me I'm a waste of life! Fight with me!*" I begged. "*Please, Tennyson, fight with me! It's what we* do. *It's what we've always done!*"

He stood up but made no move to confront me. Instead he looked at me and shook his head, like he did when I didn't get the punch line of a joke. "Things are good, Brontë," he said. "Things are great. For all of us. Why do you want to mess with it?"

I tried to answer him, but how can you find words for what you're *not* feeling?

"Fine," he said. "If you want to fight, let's fight." Then he reached out his hand and gently nudged my shoulder. "Okay," he said. "Your turn."

But instead of nudging him back, I found myself throwing my arms around him, hugging him tightly, suddenly needing the kind of closeness we must have once shared in the womb.

"What's that for?" he asked.

"I don't know . . . I don't know. . . ." All I knew is that I wanted to cry and I couldn't, and it made me want to cry all the more.

60) ILLUMINATION

If your heart tells you something but your mind tells you something else, which do you believe? Both are just as apt to lie. In fact, they play at deceit all the time. Mostly they balance each other, giving us that crucial reality check. But what happens on the rare occasions when they conspire together?

Things are good, Brontë.

And Tennyson was right. My heart told me that life was better than ever, and my mind told me not to think too deeply or all might be lost. Between my heart and mind there was a strong argument to eat my mom's first truly homemade meal in months, then slip beneath my comfortable quilt and dream peacefully till morning.

But we all have a fail-safe, don't we? When our heart and mind fails us, we have our gut. And my gut told me that if I didn't question things tonight, I never would. So after dinner

I quietly left the kitchen, counted the paces to the guest room, and pushed open the door into darkness.

Brew was under his covers, but I knew he wasn't asleep. I turned on the light.

"I want to know what's happening in this house. And God help you, Brew, if you lie to me."

He rolled over to face me, squinting in the sudden illumination. "Everything will be okay," he said. "Whatever's wrong, you'll feel better by morning."

But I already knew that. That was the problem. Right now I could feel the turmoil inside me clearing out like smoke through an open window; but as long as I could keep generating it faster than it could escape, I had the upper hand.

"Tell me!" I demanded.

He sat up. "Are you sure you really want to know?"

I nodded, even though I was feeling less sure by the second.

He stood, went over to the door, and closed it. "Why don't I show you?" Then he slowly began to unbutton his shirt.

You think you want to know the secrets of the universe. You think you want to see the way things all fit together. You believe in your heart of hearts that enlightenment will save the world and set you free.

Maybe it will.

But the path to enlightenment is rarely a pleasant one.

* * *

When the last button had been undone, Brew parted his shirt to reveal a battered torso that barely looked like flesh at all. Bruise upon bruise upon bruise. Purple and yellow, swollen red, bloodless white. His chest, his shoulders, his back. It looked like he had been thrashed by chains and bashed by bats, and pummeled by countless other blunt objects. This was worse than anything his uncle had ever done. I could see where he had masked the marks on his neck and face with covering makeup much more skillfully applied than the day he came to school with a black eye. This time you couldn't even notice it. I'm sure there wasn't an inch of his body that didn't bear some kind of damage. All of it was fresh; all of it came long after his uncle had died.

"Who did this to you?"

He pointed to one discoloration on his shoulder. "This is your father's. When he fell on the basketball court." Then he pointed to another. "This is Tennyson's from lacrosse." And then another. "This is yours; I'm not sure from where."

But I knew.

"Someone opened their car door into me . . . ," I said numbly.

He nodded and kept on going, pointing to the marks on his body like one might point out constellations in the sky. "This is Joe Crippendorf's. . . . This is Hannah Garcia's. . . . This is Andy Beaumont's. . . ." On and on he went, reciting a litany that I thought would never end. He seemed to know where every single injury had come from—maybe not how or when, but he always knew who; and I thought back to something he had said. *"I like your friends,"* he had told me. Until that moment it had never occurred to me that, for Brewster Rawlins, the cost of friendship was exacted in flesh.

". . . This is Amanda Milner's. . . . This is Matt Goldman's. . . ."

I wanted to shed all the tears in the world for him, but I couldn't. My tears were already taken away from me. My tears were filling *his* eyes instead of mine—and that's when I knew how much further this went than flesh and bone.

Then he took my hand and pressed it firmly to the center of his chest until I could feel his heart beating against my palm.

"And this . . . ," he said, ". . . this is your parents' divorce."

I pulled my hand away as if he had thrust it in hot coals. "No! They're not getting divorced! They worked things out! They're happy!"

He offered me a slim but satisfied smile, then said with absolute certainty:

"I know."

61) IMPLOSION

I ran from him.

It was callous of me; it was cowardly; it was worse than the time he ran from me when I was most vulnerable. But, like Brew, I'm human. All I knew was that I had to get to a place far enough away for me to truly know my own feelings and grapple with them. I couldn't let Brew make peace for me. I had to make peace for myself. *With* myself. Only after I was out in the street and off of our block did worry, doubt, and anger begin to filter back in. Not enough to overwhelm me, but certainly enough to give some depth of field to my vision.

My feet were on autopilot—I didn't even know where I was going until I got there.

The pool.

It was getting toward nine o'clock. The pool closed to the

public at eight, but the underwater lights came on at dusk and didn't turn off until sunrise. The gate was locked, but I knew the pool as well as I knew my own home. There were half a dozen ways to get in that didn't involve the gate; and although I had no bathing suit, I knew the storeroom door was never locked. Neither was the lost-and-found bin, which was always full of suits.

Diving into a pool as smooth as glass and creating the first ripples has always been magic to me. Like taking the first steps into virgin snow. This is what I needed—just me and my own liquid universe. I hit the water, feeling the chill. I set out to do twenty warm-up laps but quickly lost count as my head went into defragment mode, trying to put together the events of the past weeks in some meaningful way.

I wanted my frustration and my anger to align in a single direction—like a beam I could aim at someone, fry them in blame, and be done with it. But who? Not Brew—he didn't choose his gift. Not Tennyson—he didn't start this. Not my parents—they were unwitting victims with no idea where their sunny, distorted dispositions had come from.

And then there was me.

Was I to blame for bringing Brew out of his shell and exposing him to all the toxic things the rest of us carry in our souls? And as our family rose out of our own gloom, how could I not have known the cause? Me! The girl who always prided herself on her ability to see to the heart of things—to pull the truth from the tiniest bit of emotional evidence.

There could be only one answer.

I *did* know.

Maybe not consciously, but somewhere deep down I must have known that Brew was filtering out all those wounds we couldn't see. I let it happen because I *wanted* it to happen. I wanted my world to be safe and whole at all costs. I used Brew—just as Tennyson used him, just as Cody used him, just as his uncle had used him. In the end, blame didn't shine on an individual. It was a floodlight cast on all of us.

And all because we longed for healing and happiness—as if happiness is a state of being. But it's not. Happiness is a vector. It's *movement*. Like my own momentum across the pool, joy can only be defined by the speed at which you're moving away from pain.

Certainly our family could reach a place of absolute, unchangeable bliss at Brew's expense; but the moment we arrived, the moment we stopped moving, joy would become as stagnant and hopeless as perpetual despair. Happily ever after? What a curse to have to endure!

Time doesn't move at the same pace when I'm swimming, so there was no telling how long I swam. More than half an hour, less than two. Maybe. By the time I was done, I had found a sense of balance to all my emotions. I knew there had to be a way to hold on to them even in Brew's presence. There had to be. Uncle Hoyt had done it. I'd never seen a man so angry, and he held his anger even with Brew around him every day.

As I climbed out of the pool, my inner balance didn't do much for my outer balance. All those laps had tired my legs and made me just a little bit dizzy. I found myself leaning a bit too far back; I overcompensated, and then my feet slipped off the ladder rungs.

I fell into the pool, but never felt myself hit the water.

Instead, I felt my head hit the concrete edge, knocking me unconscious. And in that instant, everything—happiness, sorrow, peace, and anger—were all snuffed silent in the implosion.

BREWSTER

62) SWORDSMANSHIP

(I)

I did not choose this gift.

I cannot help what I am, what I do,

I do not choose to rob others of their pain.

At best I can mold it, and even direct it,

Use it myself, before others use me.

I have made that my secret aim,

But confessing to Brontë,

Scars me like acid rain,

Leaving me to drown.

In its rising waters,

As she leaves.

And in that moment,

I see my own glaring truth,

Her gift to me, there in her eyes.

You brought us a new light,

But that light is false.
So is darkness better
Than a heartfelt lie?
There's a rift,
Deep in my soul,
Between what I wish
And what I've become,
The anger begins to swell,
All my own and no one else's,
At the stark, undeniable truth,
That my brand of healing
Brings only misery.
I am defeated,
I am lost.
She leaves,
The door slams,
Mobilizing Tennyson.
He comes down to my room,
To find out what he has missed.
He sees my ruined back, chest, and arms.
"Put on your shirt," he says, and tosses it to me.
"Sorry," I tell him, *"I know I look horrible."*
"No," he says, *"it's cold, that's all."*
I slip the shirt back on.
"Thanks."
I have to admit

Tennyson has changed
Since the first time I met him,
For the better, but also for the worse.
He's much kinder, more honorable somehow,
But humbled by an addiction to painkillers.
We both know that painkiller is me.
"She hates me now," I tell him.
"She'll get over it," he says,
"I'll go after her—"
"No!" he says,
And in his eyes
A certain disquiet
A distinct desperation
At the thought of me leaving,
Clear evidence of the addiction.
And he looks away, hiding his shame,
But I'm more ashamed than him,
Because I made him this way.
I am not what he needs.
Not what *they* need.
"So," he asks,
"Will you stay?"
Meaning much more
Than just tonight or tomorrow,
Or this week or next.
"Should I?"

He looks away again.

"Yes . . . ," he says, then adds,

"But I don't know if it's really me talking."

I nod, an understanding reached.

"I'm going out to find her,

To make things right,"

Or at least

Properly wrong.

(II)

Alone with my own thoughts,

Searching through a chilly night,

Full of memories. . . .

When I was five years old,

I spent a week in the hospital

For three broken ribs and internal bleeding,

Because our dog was hit by a car,

And I took his pain away.

Mom had to lie and say I was the one hit,

And as I lay there recovering, she told me a story

About the world's greatest warrior,

Who could take on armies single-handedly.

The gods feared his power,

So they gave him a diamond sword,

Which fused to his fighting hand.

And every blow he struck
Would come back upon him.
Until he realized that the only way to win
Was not to fight.
When I came home from the hospital,
Our dog went to a good family,
And we never had a pet again.

> *Where would Brontë go,*
> *To be alone with her thoughts?*
> *One more place to look . . .*

When I was eight, my teacher had pneumonia
Only she never knew.
My fever climbed so high, I hallucinated;
My fingers were glittering diamond daggers
That everyone wanted for themselves.
Once my fever broke,
My mother and I had a serious talk.
"Guard your heart," she told me. ·
"That is your hero's sword."

> *I approach the pool,*
> *There's something in the water,*
> *And it's not moving. . . .*

I was ten at my mother's funeral.
Uncle Hoyt stood beside Cody and me,
His arm was on my shoulder,
He told me it would all be all right,
He would always take care of us,
He would protect us,
Protect me,
And I loved him for it.
I almost died a month later
From a kidney infection that began as Uncle Hoyt's
And quickly became mine instead.
That's how he learned what I can do,
That's when his drinking became a problem,
Because his guilt consumed him,
And he resented me for it.

Brontë's in the pool,
Facedown in the cold water.
I can't stop screaming.

(III)

How long?
I heard a splash as I approached.
Didn't I? Didn't I?
And the water's still rippling.
Maybe there's time.

NEAL SHUSTERMAN   310

I lean over the edge,
But she's too far away,
"Help! Somebody help!"
But there's no one but me.
And I can't swim.
Denying my fear,
I leap into deadly water.
My legs kick, my arms flail,
My head bobs down, then up, then down,
Coughing, spitting in the face of gravity.
I kick off my shoes,
And somehow I stay afloat,
By sheer force of will.
Closer now,
Almost there,
She's just out of reach.
My head stays above water,
But something's wrong.
Why is my chest so heavy?
Why can't I breathe?
If I'm finally swimming, why can't I breathe?
And suddenly I know!

> *Take it away.*
> *Take it away, boy.*
> *This is your purpose.*
> *Take it away!*

63) INTERFACE

Pulling you from the water won't be enough, but I can defy your fate,

I have one last gift for you, Brontë, and it's one you can't refuse.

Inches from you now, I stop kicking, let my arms relax.

They drift down to my side and the sword falls free,

Because the only way to win is not to fight.

And I'm ready for victory's embrace.

She starts to revive, I start to let go,

Giving myself to the waters,

Sinking deeper, deeper,

Faceup, eyes open,

Eyes on her.

Then she stirs the shimmering interface between life and death,

and she finally climbs out of the pool far, far above.

She doesn't see me; she doesn't know,

And it can be no other way.

I feel no wounds now,
Or any stolen pain.
All that remains
Is gratitude
And pure
Perfect
Joy.

TENNYSON

64) RECLAMATION

If he dies, I swear I'll never forgive him. I'll never forgive myself.

He's heavy as granite at the bottom of the pool, his mass so dense he doesn't float. Brontë and I struggle with every ounce of our strength to raise him to the surface.

My choice to follow him from our house wasn't out of the purest of motives. I was too much of a wimp to face the emotional wreckage that was sure to come once Brew left and the effect of his presence wore off. I wanted to stay in range— even if only at the edge of it, trailing a block behind him as he searched for my sister. Tonight I was his personal stalker.

When I got to the pool, Brontë was just climbing out. She was dazed, unsure of what had happened. I climbed the fence. I would have moved faster if I'd known. We didn't see him for at least another ten seconds. Ten seconds can make the difference between living and dying.

Our first attempt to bring him up fails. We come to the surface, gasp a breath of air, and go down again. I get beneath him, pushing him up, while Brontë grabs him in a cross-chest carry, kicking for all she's worth.

We pull him to the surface at last, somehow getting him over to the side. Standing at the edge, it takes both Brontë and me pulling on his lifeless hands to get him out of the pool.

"You learned CPR in lifesaving, right?" I ask her.

Brontë nods and begins CPR right away, frantically working on him.

"You're going too fast!"

"I never had to do it for real!"

She slows down. Two rescue breaths, thirty chest compressions.

"I'll call for help!" But when I pull out my phone, its screen is a jumble of flickering garbage. It traveled with me to the bottom of the pool, and now it's useless.

Two breaths, thirty compressions, over and over. Brontë's tears are explosive without Brew to take them away, and I'm terrified that it might mean he's already gone.

"Get out the heart paddles!" Brontë shouts. "There's a defibrillation kit somewhere in the storeroom. I saw it once, but I don't know where."

I race to the storeroom while Brontë keeps counting out chest compressions. ". . . nine, ten, eleven—damn it, Brew, breathe!"

I ransack the room—hurling things to the ground, dumping out cabinets until I find the kit—and race back to the pool deck.

"... twenty-five, twenty-six, twenty-seven ..."

I kneel beside her and get the thing open. The lid is filled with too many instructions to read. "What do I do?"

"They never showed us!" But then she reaches over and flips the On switch. Simple enough so far. A red light comes on. I can hear it charging up as I grab the heart paddles. Then a green ready light comes on. I press the metallic surface of the paddles to his chest. Brontë leaps back an instant before I press the red buttons on the paddles, and Brew's back stiffens in a violent arch.

"You're supposed to yell '*CLEAR!*'" she shouts.

"I forgot!"

I wait for it to recharge, watching for the green light, trying to relive every medical TV show I've ever seen to make sure I do this right.

Brontë puts two fingers against his neck and shakes her head: no pulse.

Brew has got to fight his way back—but he won't. He can't. He's not a fighter; it's not in his nature.

But it is in mine! If Brewster won't fight, then I'll have to fight for him.

"*CLEAR!*"

A second jolt. His back arches. Still no pulse.

"It's not working," wails Brontë. "It's no use."

But today failure is not an option.

As I wait for the machine to recharge, I look into his half open, unseeing eyes, and I realize that CPR and heart paddles are not enough. He needs something more from us.

"We have to take it back!" I tell Brontë. I don't even know what I mean yet. It's not a thought; it's a feeling—something I'm trying to put into words, knowing I don't have much time to do it.

"Take what back?" Brontë asks

Then the understanding hits me. What Brew needs—what WE need. The only way to save him. It's simple, and yet it's impossible. But no more impossible than the things Brew has already done.

"We have to take all of it back! Everything we let him take away! We have to steal it back from him."

I see in her eyes the moment she gets it. "How?"

And suddenly I flash to Uncle Hoyt. "How did his uncle stay angry? Because he *wanted* to. The things we gave to Brew—we have to want them. We have to OWN them!"

Brontë nods. The light turns green. "One last time," she says.

I press the paddles to his chest, but my thoughts aren't on those paddles. Instead they're on the body bruises I gave away, the head trips I refused to take, the pangs of sorrow I so easily handed over. Against my own self-preservation instinct, I fight to feel those things I refused to feel before.

"*CLEAR!*"

I pump him full of electricity while trying to steal back a fraction of what I never should have given him in the first place. The battering he stole for me on the field. The heartache he spared me at home. Once I started to give just a little bit of it to him, it was easy to give it all away. But no matter how hard it is, I'm ready to take it all back if it will save him. All of it and more. So I silently pray that I might feel the hurt again somewhere, anywhere, *everywhere*.

Brontë checks his pulse again. "Nothing."

But *I* feel something. There's a tiny ache on my upper arm. It's the spot where Brontë had punched me so angrily that day of my lacrosse game. When I raise my arm, I see the faintest bit of a yellow bruise that wasn't there a moment ago. All I was able to reclaim from Brewster was a single bruise . . .

. . . and that's all it takes.

"Wait!" says Brontë. "I think I have a pulse!"

Suddenly he coughs, water gushing out of his mouth. Brontë and I both scream in grateful surprise. We roll him to one side, water still spilling out of him. He coughs again. His eyes flutter open, and then they close.

We saved you, Brew! We saved you! And right now at this moment nothing else in the world matters to Brontë, or to me. We saved you!

But he's not waking up.

With no phone, my feet are the only means of communication with the outside world. Brontë holds his head in her lap as I race to the nearest house, pounding on the door, refusing to leave until they let me in.

Brew still hasn't woken when I come back with help. He's still unconscious when the ambulance comes to take him away—and the sense of urgency on the faces of the paramedics says everything they won't say out loud. Something isn't right.

We saved you, Brew. We brought you back. So why won't you wake up?

65) PAINLESS

Cody sits on a bench, his face twisted in disgust as he watches all the other kids at Roosevelt Children's Home play on a ridiculously elaborate jungle gym.

"It's not fair," Cody whines.

"It's your own stupid fault," I remind him.

He grabs one of his crutches and jabs me in the foot. "That's for calling me stupid!"

Brontë and I visit him at the home a few times each week. Actually, we're both volunteering here—they roped us in after the second or third time. They're good at that. Now that lacrosse season is over, it's something to do. Besides, it looks good on college applications.

"I can climb to the first platform, can't I? It's not that high."

"If you do," says Brontë, "they won't let you come out here at all."

He punches his cast in frustration, and it gives off a dull thud like a mannequin leg. It's a nasty cast, going all the way from his ankle to his thigh.

"I hate it!" he says. "And it always itches!"

There were too many questions surrounding Brew's near drowning. Enough questions that Child Protective Services saw fit to reevaluate us as a foster family and took Cody back. I wasn't there when he broke his leg, but the accident report tells a pretty clear story. Cody was in his social worker's office being evaluated. Then, the moment he was told that he wouldn't be coming back to live with us, he went ballistic and jumped out of the second-floor window into a tree—which might have been all right if he didn't totally miss the tree.

He broke his leg in three places.

"You're a very lucky boy," the doctors told him, but I don't think he sees it that way. Cody's a kid who will go through life learning things the hard way. But it looks like this is one of life's major lessons that's going to stick.

Dad picks us up in the reception area at five to take Brontë, Cody, and me over to the hospital. Sometimes it's Mom, sometimes it's Dad, but never both. Dad moved back into the guest room shortly after Cody left. Negotiations between our parents have stalled. Silence and fast food have returned.

There's a nurse in Brew's hospital room when we enter, checking his chart. "Always good to see you," she says with a smile, and leaves us to our visit.

Cody hobbles on his crutches to a chair beside Brew's bed, plops himself down, and starts reciting for Brew a blow-by-blow description of everything that's happened in the Universe of Cody in the three days since he was last here. He doesn't pause for a response since he's used to not getting one.

On the wall behind Brew's bed are pictures drawn by Cody. A silver Mylar GET WELL SOON balloon floats lazily up from the foot of his bed, and will probably be there until the end of time, since those things never lose air. On a table are wilting flowers that Brontë replaces with some fresh ones. Next to the flower vase is a lacrosse MVP trophy.

Brew lies on the bed, eyes closed, connected to devices that looked intimidating at first but that we've gotten used to seeing. An electroencephalograph, a heart rate monitor, an IV, and one machine that lets off random, unpredictable pings like it's sonar checking for enemy submarines.

Brontë sits down and massages his fingers.

"He looks good," says Dad.

I guess everything is relative. All of his bruises are gone, although there are some scars that I suspect will never fade entirely. He's peaceful, and takes away none of the pain we feel as we linger by his bedside. Nor does he feel any pain of his own.

If it was a mistake to keep him alive, then I take full responsibility. I admit my selfishness of not wanting to lose the strangest, and maybe the best, friend I've ever had. Blame me for forcing him to linger like this. I accept all guilt, because I'm not the kind of person who gives in. I'm not wired that way.

In a while Dad goes to move the car out of the twenty-minute zone. But the rest of us stay a while longer.

"When Brew wakes up," Cody says, "I'm keeping my broken leg—just like I kept my scaredness when we was up on the electrical tower."

And I believe he *could* keep his broken leg. It's amazing the things you can hold on to when you're determined to keep them, and the immunity you can develop if you truly want to. I know that Brontë and I have been working on our immunity—doing our best to *want* all those unpleasant things we might otherwise give away.

On the way out, we stop by the nurses' station. "Has there been any change?" Brontë asks. "Anything at all?"

"Well," says one of the nurses, "we keep seeing unusual spikes in his brain waves. The fact that there's any activity at all is a very good sign."

"How good?" Brontë asks.

The nurse camouflages a sigh with a warm smile. "Honey, people can be in comas for months or years. Sometimes they wake up without explanation, and sometimes they don't. As much as we know about the brain, it's nothing compared to what we *don't* know."

It's a speech the nurse has got memorized—in fact, she told us the exact same thing two weeks before. I can't fault her for giving us a canned response—it's her job. Still, I'm feeling obnoxious enough to finish it for her. "'But there are new discoveries every day,'" I say, repeating back to her what she said the last time we were here—what she must say to everyone waiting for a loved one to regain consciousness. "'Maybe we can be the ones who win a Nobel Prize for unlocking the mysteries of the brain someday.'"

Rather than taking my mocking personally, she sigh-smiles again. "Definitely a sign that I need a vacation," she says.

"But if he does wake up," says Brontë, "you'll call us, won't you? Promise me that you'll call!"

"I promise," says the nurse. "We've got your number."

"We've got *all* of their numbers," says another nurse.

"Memorized!" says a third.

Maybe we're the ones who need a vacation.

66) HELLO

On a mockingly bright Memorial Day weekend, when everyone else celebrates a day off from work and school, Mom and Dad sit Brontë and me down in the kitchen for a serious conversation. We know what it's about before they start talking. We know because the two gray suitcases are up from the basement and have been side by side in the guest room for days.

"Your mother and I have decided it's time for me to move out," Dad says. They are words Brontë and I have been dreading for so long, I can't recall when the dread began.

"It's just for a while," Mom says, but that's like closing the barn door after the lawyers have fled.

Brontë's tears come quickly. "Don't lie to us. There *is* no 'just for a while.'"

Our parents' eyes have become shiny and wet as well. "Maybe you're right," Dad says. "Maybe it's forever. Maybe."

It's the F word that gets my waterworks going. *Forever.* The escape valve opens; I wipe my eyes quickly and close the valve again. Forever sucks.

While Brontë gets herself under control I say, "Things will probably get worse before they get better."

"Tennyson's right," says Brontë. "And we'll probably both have bizarre meltdowns every once in a while, even if we seem okay."

"Yeah," I say, and add, "If we *don't* have meltdowns, that's when you should worry."

Our parents look at us with the stupefied kind of amazement that's usually reserved for slot machine jackpots, or papal introductions.

"How did you two get to be such old souls?" says Dad, incredulous.

Without missing a beat I say, "Prolonged sun exposure," and pinch crow's-feet into the corners of my eyes.

"Yeah," says Brontë. "We'll probably need Botox at twenty-two."

And in spite of the seriousness of the day, Mom and Dad can't help but chuckle.

It's only after they leave the room that it truly begins to hurt. I hold Brontë—not just to comfort her, but to comfort myself as well, because maybe I'm feeling as awful as she is, whether I show it or not.

But in that bottomless moment when the whole world feels like it's tearing in half, I realize deep down that this is the moment we've been waiting for since the day Brew fell silent. We've finally come back around to where things were when we took Brewster and Cody Rawlins into our home . . .

. . . which means this is the moment that we have finally, *truly* taken back our own pain.

That day at the pool we could only bring Brew halfway back—he needed something more to complete the journey home. But now we've finally taken full possession of what is rightfully ours, because everyone must feel their own pain— and as awful as that is, it's also wonderful . . .

. . . because isn't that the sound of a phone ringing?

Not just one, but all of them. Our house phone here in the kitchen, Brontë's cell phone up in her room, Mom's in her purse—for all I know every phone in the world is ringing at that very moment. But there's one ring in particular that grabs my attention.

In the kitchen junk drawer sits my old waterlogged cell phone, which I never had the chance to replace. It hasn't worked since the day it journeyed with me to the bottom of the pool—but as I open the drawer, there it is, playing a familiar ringtone, its call light blinking as magically and impossibly bright as a firefly.

Like me, Brontë looks at it with awe, and a little bit of fear—because there are some things you simply know. Miles beyond intuition, and one step past a leap of faith, there are some things you know!

"Answer it," she says.

But instead I put it into her hands and smile.

"I think it's for you."

As she moves the phone to her ear, I can already feel our spirits rising with anticipation—amazed at how quickly that can happen after our parents' news. I've always been a rational guy. I believe what I can see, but now I also believe there is room in the world for miracles. Maybe not the ones we expect, but they're miracles all the same. They happen every day if only we pay attention.

"Hello?" says Brontë into a phone that shouldn't work—and the smile on her face, the sudden joy in her eyes tell me everything I need to know. Yes, today is a day for our family to grieve, but now it's also a day to rejoice!

So open your eyes, Brew. Open your eyes, and talk to us. We'll keep our pain, but I promise we'll share our joy. Talk to us, Brew . . . because we're finally ready to take your call.